VAMPIRE-ISH

A Hypochondriac's Tale

Candi Teasdale

MILLRACE ROAD MEDIA

Paperback:
ISBN-978-1-7352331-8-5

To all the Blood Bankers

1

PARANOIA

"NO HUMAN CONDITION IS EVER PERMANENT."
—SOCRATES

I never comprehended these words. I figured he talked about death or about the improvement of one's self. But now I consider an alternative—he actually knew something the rest of us didn't.

My love for the philosophies of life, which I've studied over my epigrammatic college career, led me to a new conclusion: "Socrates must have known about vampires."

Philosophy had very little to do with my day-to-day life. I tried to apply my philosophical beliefs, become a better human, and understand my place and purpose in life, but a painful reality still existed—my nagging paranoia.

Pretty early on, my allergies became a problem. My over-protective mother self-diagnosed every ailment and brought with her a fear that I may die from everything. My father, who always wanted me to be the next star cornerback, viewed my bubble life as a dismal disappointment. But all my allergy shots, hypochondria, and Benadryl couldn't excuse one thing—my basic failure at being human.

Throughout the years, and the countless doctors, I learned to face my phobias and manage my allergies. I discovered spinach and vitamins and Socrates. I joined a few organizations and read my fair share of pamphlets. But as prepared as I was to face my personal downfalls, I was not prepared for this.

I remember very specifically the event that altered my perception of the world I knew. The day before was much like all the other afternoons that ran together; taking for granted the seemingly dull activities that filled my time on my day off. I remember watching mind-numbing sports, going down to the fresh market, and stopping by the corner drug store to pick up a few general prescriptions: Prednisone, Naproxen for the headaches, Clonazepam, Pamelor, which I switched to after using Zoloft, a replacement Epi-pen—stupid Chinese restaurant, and a new antibiotic, one I hoped would not counteract any of the others. Just a few drugs; this was a good week.

Dr. Heckenliable didn't like me very much, and I couldn't blame him. I think he gave me the drugs, in part, to keep me out of his hair. However, Dr. Yung, my therapist, thought exercise might help combat the depression and solve some of my anxiety issues. I must state that I always knew running outside was a bad idea. Prescribed exercise didn't sound very healthy either, and the thought of going to a gym sounded close to hell. My lack of knowledge regarding anything gym equipment related, not to mention my scrawny body, are just a few of the reasons for my hesitation. Personally though, I blame my father and his high hopes for me to carry on the football tradition. I couldn't enter that world without thinking of his disappointment. But, within the lines of healthy thinking, I decided to start recreational running.

I popped a few pills into my mouth and swirled them around with Mountain Dew before setting off on my first attempt at a morning jog. I stuffed my inhaler in my pocket, just in case. I hadn't had an asthma attack since I moved to the city but felt better feeling it jingle around in my shorts. I plugged my headphones into my old iPod, turning on some post rock. Post rock—good for the soul—I hoped it might make me feel better about my insane decision to get out of bed in the first place.

Dr. Heck had advised me to go running early in the morning before the sun warmed everything; the sun peaked early in New York, but it had not yet pierced through the thick trees of Central Park, still hovering near the horizon. I lived down 66th, close to the Hunter College campus, and one of the best locations in New York City if I wanted to run in the park, I've heard. The cool air helped me to go farther. Everyone hates the first mile, right?

I headed toward my favorite grove of trees, a shady patch close to the East Meadow, perfect for deep contemplations after a long lecture. All of a sudden, from out of nowhere, a force hit the left side of my body, sending me to the ground. I staggered back to my feet confused, searching for what hit me. I checked my side—a little scrape on my elbow, but nothing I couldn't shake off.

I know I'm a grown man, but I must admit I was a little freaked out. My first time running in Central Park and I get mugged? Seriously?

My eyes scoured the darkness for something, anything, in the shadows. I should be alone, but something moved between the trees. I couldn't believe what I spotted—a young teenage girl cowering by a bush. Maybe a runaway, I thought. Regardless, she was a sad little waif, a desperate soul, lost and bewildered in the shadows. Had the poor thing tried to mug me? At a better glance, I immediately thought "this girl needs rehab," what with the sunken eyes, white skin, and hollow expression. She could easily pass for a ghost or a zombie if I hadn't thought better of it.

But as I stood there staring stupidly at the girl trying to figure out what she wanted from me, she jumped toward me, almost cat-like, as if pouncing on its prey. I quickly shoved her away, like brushing off a mosquito. What a bizarre thing to do. If she wanted my iPod *that* badly, she could have it. I'd wanted to upgrade anyway. Besides, I'd feel bad for anyone desperate enough to take my iPod—it didn't even have a touch screen.

Against my better judgment, I turned away from her and continued running on the well-worn path, hoping she would just go home and forget about the iPod.

No sooner had I turned around, she came at me, from behind this time.

"Geez, girl," I shouted, flipping her away. "I'm not carrying any money if you're that desperate!" She actually did look that desperate. My cousin Zane, on my mother's side, was a heroin addict. I knew enough to recognize the signs.

But her eyes shifted, and she smiled impishly. "I might be, but not for money," she said out of the corner of her mouth.

This is insane, I thought in my head. I ditched her again and ran even faster than before. This time, I headed off the trail more in public view, in case any other insane person might be out running this early too. But before I crested a hill toward the East Meadow, it happened. She lunged, straddling her legs around me like a piggy-back rider. A sharp pain entered my neck. I flexed my arms, and she dropped. A sharp pain shot through the right side of my neck. My hand reached up and I felt the blood. What did that crazy girl do, bite me? Thoughts immediately swirled around in my head of all the horrifying possibilities of infection that could be entering my bloodstream, and not knowing one thing about this girl's sexual history, I panicked.

I turned to confront the girl but hesitated.

What was wrong with her? Was she puking? As I looked closer, I noticed her spitting out blood, *my* blood, from her mouth.

"What is wrong with you?" she yelled, wiping her mouth.

"What do you mean *me*?" I yelled back as I approached. "*You're* the crazy lunatic that attacked me!"

A somewhat smile crossed her face. "Guess I deserve it," she muttered, while wiping her mouth. "Never thought I'd want to drink water again; I need to wash out my mouth."

As I approached her, preparing to rip her apart with my unbridled language, I got a better glimpse of her pathetic, wasted self. She looked as if she wore her soul on the outside of her skin. I had never seen anyone so pale and pasty white. Almost anemic. What a lack of vitamin D. Maybe her insides were wasting away, as if she had . . .

A severe panic swelled inside me. What *had* this girl been doing out here in Central Park at night? Was she a druggy, or a pathetic homeless waif, and in Manhattan? What if she had . . . Oh NO! Not that . . . anything but that. Can I get it from being tasted?

I ran. I didn't look back. I had to call my doctor. Dr. Heckenliable would know; he would know what to do. My stomach began to turn. I think my nerves were starting to get the better of me. And then my vision began to blur. Did HIV work this fast? I could be dead by noon if that were true. I wished I had gotten some of the girl's blood, just in case, like you do with a poisonous snake. Could they make antivenin for this?

Memories grew fuzzy on exactly how I got back to my apartment. I felt the newly contracted virus burning through my body exploring its new host. Nothing could be as bad as this.

How wrong I was.

Someone slapped me. Was someone calling my name?

"Ollie. Come on, Oliver. Wake up!"

Another slap and I opened my eyes. Why was it so bright? I looked around. Mitch, my best friend and nemesis combined, was the one slapping me around. We'd been friends forever, though so long, neither one of us really knew why we were still friends. He ate all my food, messed up my house, and dated girls who had dumped me. He had never been a very good friend.

"Ollie, you look like hell. What happened to you?"

I slowly sat up and shook my head. It hurt. Heavy pangs of pressure pressed against my temples. I hated headaches like this. I needed my Naproxen. For a brief moment, I thought I had dreamed the whole thing. Maybe I had fallen back asleep and hadn't gone on my morning run after all. But as soon as I lifted my hand, I saw the dried blood and slowly freaked out.

"Ollie!" Mitch grabbed my arm before I could scream again. "Where have you been? You didn't answer your cell phone…" he trailed off. "Dude, what happened to your neck?"

The feeling, like raw, carnal anger, ignited somewhere inside. I felt nauseous and went to the bathroom to see the damage; a bright purple bruise sat vividly on my neck. I washed the blood off, revealing the tiny tears in my flesh where that girl . . . yuck. I dry heaved.

"Ollie, come on!" Mitch came in and saw the gash. "Man, did you get stabbed? Cool. Does that explain where you've been for three days?"

"What? Three days? I talked to you yesterday."

"You mean Saturday. Dude, it's Tuesday."

I checked my watch. My digital calendar confirmed this. "Why didn't you come over before?"

Mitch shrugged as he ate a donut. "But that looks infected, dude." Small bits of donut came flying out of his mouth as he spoke.

Three days? I was so confused. If I really had been out for three days, that means I didn't show up for... Oh no. What was I going to tell my boss? What about class? How was I going to explain where I've been? Three days. Really?

And Mitch was right, I did look like hell, like I'd been punched in the face a few times. My eyes looked swollen and purple, and I looked like I had lost weight, a good ten pounds gone. Even my slightly olive skin looked gray in the florescent bathroom light. I looked like a walking, talking corpse.

In that moment, my anxiety came rushing in. I needed to call my doctor. I needed to go to work. I needed my Clonazepam.

"Sorry, were you going to eat this?" Mitch asked of the half-eaten donut in his mouth.

Strange. After three days I didn't want to eat anything. I just wanted the poison out of my body. "No, eat it. I'll go take my meds with some crackers or something."

By my small apartment sink, the sun streamed through the tiny separation between the homemade curtains and grazed my skin.

"Youch!" It burned. I pulled my ugly checkered cloth over the window. It shouldn't be *that* warm yet—it was only April.

I shook out a few pills and grabbed a glass of water. I tossed the pills into my mouth, but before I could get the water to my lips, I knew there was something immediately wrong. I spit out everything in the sink. They tasted like poison.

I rechecked all the labels. Everything looked the same. Maybe my new Pamelor had given me some weird side effect. But I had been taking it for a few weeks now, and nothing like this had ever happened before. I rechecked the antibiotic. "Ah crap. I knew it."

"What?" Mitch looked up out of the fridge.

"Sulfa. TMP Sulfa? Right there on the label!" I threw the bottle in the trash. "I'm allergic to Sulfa, I think. I mean, I might be."

"Huh? I don't get it. How could you be allergic to the sofa?"

I ignored him and within minutes was on the phone with my doctor explaining my puzzling reaction. Something was going on. I wanted to get tested for everything.

"Are you going to tell me what happened to you?" Mitch asked. "It has to be a cool story, like you got stabbed with a fork or a prong or something—"

"It's a bite mark, you idiot."

"From a squirrel?"

"Yeah, that makes sense," I said, still in my head as I grabbed my hoodie from the hook. I looked outside again, pulled up my hood, placed my regular glasses in the wide pocket, and put on my prescription sunglasses. "Sulfa reactions can cause sensitivity to the sun."

"How do you know that?"

"I looked it up once. You come'n?"

Mitch grabbed another donut from the package, and we left.

I tried to stay in the shade in the taxi, moving away from the sun at each turn. Mitch kept punching me every time I moved.

"Why are you dressed like the Unabomber?"

"Just tell me what you found."

Mitch had his handheld open looking upside-effects. "Do you have a goat?"

"Huh?" I looked at his screen. "Gout. No. Let me see that." I grabbed his device and looked on Drugs.com. "TMP Sulfa," I read aloud, "Should drink plenty of water. Well, that's a problem. Here we go: loss of appetite, nausea, sensitivity to sun, skin rashes, anemia... I think I have all those things. It makes sense."

"No, it doesn't. Those are *side* effects." Mitch took back his phone. "That doesn't mean you are allergic."

"I can't stand the sun right now. It's burning my skin. That's why I'm keeping myself covered."

"Sensitive? You've taken one pill. Loss of appetite? You're a vegetarian. You lost your appetite a long time ago."

I didn't want to talk about it anymore.

I had completely forgotten about the desperate girl and how I had tasted so disgusting to her. I was so self-absorbed in my own world, I never once considered hers.

Dr. Heckenliable's office was so cold, I felt shivery. Luckily, they took me back within minutes. A slight, teenage-looking girl came in to draw my blood. "Where's Nadia?" I asked her. I had never seen this girl before.

"She's um… helping someone right now. My name is Jen. I'm new."

Never tell anyone you're a new phlebotomist.

She poked me and missed. She tried again and again, but no blood would come out of my veins. "Would you like me to try?" I didn't like having to be so blunt with the poor girl, but my arm started to look like a pin cushion.

The girl grimaced and left the room only to return with Nadia, the lovely RN. "Hello Ollie," her smile ran crooked and sweet up the side of her face. I had always liked Nadia, In many ways, she was why I stayed with Dr. Heck. She was witty and wicked smart; all the things I wished I could be. Our interactions were rather superficial, but I still looked forward to them. She placed a hand on her hip. "Giving my newbie a bad time, are we?"

"Giving *her* a bad time? Say that to my arm."

"Calm down. You're a big boy. Just hold still." Nadia was a good phlebotomist, but even she moved the needle around struggling to find a vein. Finally, dark red clots filled the tube. "It's coagulated," she spoke to herself as she flicked the tube.

I watched the sticky, black goo slurp down the side of the glass tube. *What is that? Out of my arm?* The memory of my attack flashed fresh in my mind. It might not be the Sulfa at all; the girl who attacked me must have had something to do with that.

"Oliver?" Nadia could tell I had gone into shock. "Are you on any new medications?"

I could hardly speak as I looked at the strange clots stuck to the side of the tube. "Well, yes, but it shouldn't do that."

She took the sample, labeled it, and left. Then we waited. And waited. Mitch and I had a good, heated argument about using a cell phone in a hospital while waiting. He wouldn't stop texting. Finally, Dr. Heck entered with a very puzzled look on his face.

I sat quietly as he examined me.

He looked in my eyes, in my mouth, my ears. He made me breath in and out as he listened. He felt my pulse. And then he looked at my neck and at the ugly bruise and tear marks that were left from where that crazed girl had tried to kill me. He scribbled something down on my chart and looked back, very calm.

"So, Doc, tell it to me straight. Was it the Sulfa?" I asked. "Or do I have AIDS? I mean, come on Doc. HIV?"

Still, he looked at me puzzled. "Sorry Oliver, you do *not* have HIV."

I was so excited, I smiled and wanted to shout, but something he had said caught my attention. "Sorry?" I repeated. "Why would you be sorry I don't have—"

"My boy." He took off his glasses and looked me square in the eye. "What you have is much worse. As far as I can tell, from everything I can see, you are essentially . . . dead."

Mitch busted out laughing. I rolled my eyes. What a stupid joke. "Really, Dr. Heck, I need to know."

"So do I," he repeated, scribbling again. "You have no pulse. Your blood is dried and clotted. You have no blood pressure. You look like you need a transfusion."

Nadia returned and handed the doctor something. The look on her face filled with both pleasure and curiosity. "These may be of help to you. Nadia here is an expert on your condition. New York has a very unique culture here. But, from here on out, I can no longer help you." He smiled wide, like he enjoyed being rid of me, and returned his glasses. "It's been a pleasure, Mr. Brixby. Best of luck to you."

He shook my hand and handed me a few pamphlets. I thumbed through them: *The Curious World of Vampirism; So, Now You're a Vampire – Accepting Your New Role in Society; Blood Facts – Dos and Don'ts.* This had to be a joke, right?

I went blank. This is the dumbest joke Mitch has ever played on me; worse than the time he wrapped up one of my own Star Wars action figures and gave it to me for Christmas. My best friend was still laughing on the floor. I looked around for the hidden cameras.

Nadia came forward, her arms folded with one eyebrow raised. "Welcome, Ollie. I must admit I'm rather surprised, but I love it when friends become a part of my family."

I felt stupid. "Does this mean I'm not allergic to Sulfa?"

"Well, you definitely do *not* have HIV." Dr. Heck added something else to his notes then handed my chart to Nadia, nodding to me as he exited.

Mitch continued to laugh.

2

THE FACTS

"DEATH MAY BE THE GREATEST OF ALL HUMAN BLESSINGS."

I waited in the office until the sun no longer slipped through the shadowing skyscrapers. It was a lot to digest in one crazy afternoon. Nadia explained a few things, but honestly, I wasn't listening. She gave me a few cards that I never looked at. All I heard was the ringing in my ears accompanied by silence from the absence of my thumping heart.

Mitch read me something in the cab and began to laugh again, but I didn't hear what, and by the time I reached my apartment and glimpsed my medication melted with the dripping water at the bottom of the sink, I snapped.

I could not recall where all the anger came from; I'm relatively rational. Many unfair things had happened to me in the past. I couldn't figure how this one was any different. But it might be possible all the years of prevention, the paranoia, all came down to nothing. Even with being so careful, calamities still prevailed. I only recognized bad things happening to me. Others, like Mitch, could slide through life on sheer luck. How fair was that?

My primal scream came from somewhere inside me I'd never let out. It echoed loudly with the crashing of the dishes Mitch had piled in the sink. Next, I dumped all my meds, starting with the antibiotic, down my disposal, grinding them into little bits. I felt evil as I laughed at the chalky powder clinking around in the sink. Take that, stupid Sulfa!

"Whoa. Whoa!" Mitch yelled at me, taking my arms in a firm grip behind my back.

"Why do you care?" I struggled with his grip. "You can't sell them for anything."

Mitch reevaluated the struggle but kept his grip. He had always been stronger than me, and tougher, more popular. Oh, I hate him. Why were we friends again?

"Gee, I thought you'd be stronger," Mitch uttered wrestling me to the couch. "Aren't vampires super strong?"

Vampire? The dreaded word. I didn't like hearing *that* word. Me? I'm just not vampire material. There had to be a mistake. I can't be a… THAT word.

After my struggle grew futile, and personally embarrassing and stupid, I sat up, over my fit, and looked at myself in my full-length mirror across the room. What an utter mess! My skin looked drained and lifeless, my hair a mess, my torn neck was now dark purple, my glasses lop-sided.

"Wait a second." My heart lifted at the words. "I can see myself! Mitch, it isn't true! I knew it! It can't be true if I can see my reflection, right?" I felt exuberant.

"Ollie, Nadia told you about that in the clinic."

"Huh?"

He threw me own of those pamphlets from the clinic, 'Fact or Fiction.' I read it aloud. The thin trifold didn't go into much detail about any of the conditions, just pointing out brief statements of what is known about vampires.

Fact: Blood is a vampire's main source of food.

Fiction: Crosses, holy water, or any other religious symbol do not harm vampires.

Fact: Vampires CAN die by wooden stakes in the heart—anyone can.

Fiction: Vampires do not need to sleep in coffins, but the more devoted prefer to.

Fact: Sunlight harms vampires as they no longer have the ability to create pigment or grow skin cells. A burn on vampire skin takes much longer to heal than normal human skin.

Fiction: Vampires do not live on Virgins alone.

On and on it read. A lot of it made practical sense. It stated clearly about mirrors, "Vampires are not imaginary, so of course they will have reflections. That is all the comfort I get."

"There is actually quite a lot of information in those pamphlets," Mitch stated, opening a bag of chips. The whole routine of him coming and stealing my food made me think.

"You sure are handling this vampire thing well."

Mitch shrugged. "It really won't be much different, I figure. It actually makes you, I don't know, cooler."

"But what if I come after your blood?"

Mitch erupted in laughter. "Did you really say that?" He nearly rolled off the couch. "You wouldn't bite me. I eat too much garlic." This was true. "And honestly, I don't think you could do it; I mean, bite someone, bite another human being. You're paranoid. You're a vegetarian. The idea of hurting animals sends you to the toilet. To suck someone's blood without multiple tests performed…" He laughed even harder.

And that about summed it up. He was absolutely right. I couldn't do it. I did get nauseous at the image. I could not live this type of lifestyle. I would be the worst vampire in history. "What am I going to do?"

"Look at this one." Mitch threw another pamphlet; it hesitated midair as it caught a brief wind and then dropped in my lap. This one was bigger than *Fact or Fiction* and I could already see the language in the pamphlet, much heavier, filled with medical jargon and terminology I didn't understand.

Un-Life: A Quick Reference for Medical and Physical Advice and Help for Living Vampires

Clinically the words "Deceased" or "Dead" would give the understanding of a state of unconsciousness in which the body no longer functions. The term "Un-Dead" gives the misnomer of a person who is in a state of consciousness, but body functions cease to operate. However, the state of the Un-dead does need substance to function much like the living.

Blood to the Un-Dead body helps oxygenate the body and give nourishment to the system without requiring the functionality of organs and tissues to process. This is the recommended method of the Un-Dead.

However, in our technologic and self-aware day and age, there are many alternatives to help with an Un-dead diet. Medications and alternative products are available to help alleviate pressures of fresh blood drainage. Some are oxygenation pills, Red Cell

Pheresis, simulated blood, herbal supplements from the Yate-yeo and Nicaraguan dog-eating trees, along with Cryptid scientific extractions from Chupacabras, Ethiopian "death birds" and the African Mamba Mutu. There are also many studies being done on further issues and advancements in Cryptozoology in the hopes to help the growing Vampire population...

"Since you like medication so much, I figured we could look into that."

For once, I was impressed, but that was lost again by the huge belch erupting from Mitch's mouth.

The other pamphlets also gave some good information, along with advice about diet, jobs, and lifestyle. I took a glance at the cards Nadia gave me:

Marcus Breinhardt – Vampire Psychiatrist

VA – Vampires Anonymous

The Cell – Underground Letting Club

Awakening Herbal and Supplemental Store Supply

and...

"Hot Topic?" I questioned.

"Yeah, Nadia mentioned that. If you sort through all the *Cartoon Network* and *Nightmare Before Christmas* stuff, you can actually find useful items."

"Like vampire teeth or striped tights?"

"More like a Sun-Shielded jacket, you ass."

I felt bad. He only tried to help. I supposed maybe later I would go online and look.

Then my phone rang, and it stunned me. I forgot about my undead life after my death. Should I answer it and continue in my previous situation? I looked at the number—Warren, my boss. I swore in my mind. I completely forget about my job.

"What do I do?" I whispered to Mitch, like the phone had already answered. His face told me nothing. I danced around a moment before my conscience won and I answered.

"Hello... Yes! Warren. Glad you called... I was going to call... Where am I? Oh, it's awful... really... I—" I looked to Mitch for help. He kept making a crinkled expression raising his fingers to his mouth like fangs. Not funny. I needed help. What did he want me to tell him? "Yes, sorry, what... yes, you see... caught a... what is that... a pig? No! Wait... I mean, I didn't catch a pig... yes, I understand. No I... Oh, I got it... Sorry, no, Warren. What I mean is, I have Swine Flu."

Phew, good one. Warren didn't argue and I was off for the rest of the week. I promised I'd fax a doctor's note to the office, which I knew Nadia would be happy to provide, and the mess was settled, at least until Monday.

3

BACON SMOOTHIES

"WORTHLESS PEOPLE LOVE ONLY TO EAT AND DRINK; PEOPLE OF WORTH EAT AND DRINK ONLY TO LIVE."

Hunger didn't come for a full day, and when it hit, it hit hard. It was a different kind of hunger, not like the tummy growling ache you get when you forget to eat breakfast. This was a sensation I'd never experienced; a longing, coursing, driving force ran around my body. My muscles ached with increasing pounding in constant throbs. I wasn't sure how to satisfy it, without, you know, the obvious.

The Un-Life pamphlet actually gave fantastic nutritional advice, like information I might find at the local GN store. And Mitch, who once told me he would rather eat an entire stick of butter than go in Whole Foods Market, went and gathered some items the pamphlet suggested might be found there. He felt rather bad about my predicament. The realization that I wouldn't be buying Doritos hit him rather hard.

In my weakness, I did try to eat real food. It was habit. But it didn't matter, I gagged on everything. How would I survive without sushi? I couldn't help but buy it. The mouthwatering tuna roll changed to an upheaval of black, sludgy goo. My body wouldn't allow it in. But more than that, the flavor altered, and there was no way I desired to taste the slime again.

My diet needed a fix, like I had been diagnosed with diabetes or high cholesterol, though this was much worse. The herbivore habits of my wheatgrass smoothie had now been changed to sucking on a raw steak. I nearly cried when I sent my Organic Goji berries down the toilet. What else could I do? They were close in expiration, and I knew Mitch wouldn't touch them.

I gathered this would be harder than going vegan. My mentality had to change; I had to think differently, or I was going to starve. I had a big problem.

So, I called the only person I could think of for help.

When Nadia arrived, everything improved. Even her presence in the room made things lift. I'd never spent any time with her outside of the clinic, but there was no one else. I figured vampires always looked like Twilight extras and acted like sullen teenagers. Nadia proved me wrong.

Nadia had spirit. She was cutting edge and stunning. I never appreciated how long her hair was, since I'd only seen her wear it up into a twist at the clinic, but it went all the way down her back and straight as an arrow, so thick and black it nearly looked blue in the shadows. With the long hair, her face looked different, more heart-shaped. Or maybe I'd never paid attention.

Mitch had been good company but didn't understand the loneliness I felt—Nadia did. That made a big difference. She organized a diet plan that helped sustain me. I made a friend on the dark side. It prompted me to ask her how it all happened.

She just shook her head. "Not such a good idea, Parker," she called me Parker after Peter Parker, AKA Spiderman, after her own theory that the medications I was on might have altered my change into vampirism, but she had yet to prove anything. "That's info I need to volunteer. Don't ask anyone; wait for them to tell you."

She finished up whatever was blending and handed it to me.

"Okay, try this."

The shake looked like nothing I'd ever want to taste.

"Are you going to explain what I taste?" I asked, seriously concerned.

A mischievous smile passed her lips. "Not yet."

It smelled really strongly of bacon. I took a very, very small taste on the tip of my tongue and was instantly impressed. A little bigger sip revealed a very strong taste of salt and something tangy I couldn't identify with a satisfying palette that didn't make me gag.

"What is in this?" I asked, taking another sip. It had been a while without any sustenance.

"It's a combination of different ingredients that make up the blood chemistry, like iron and potassium. There's salt tablets, pig's liver—which is full of blood—some cryptin herbal extracts, a few Excedrin, and a pomegranate."

"Excedrin and a pomegranate? Please explain."

Nadia laughed a little, "Weird, I know. I made this recipe myself. I figure the Excedrin opens the fluid pathways, letting the nutrients sink in faster. And pomegranates are one of the rare fruits that its acidity level does not affect our bodies. And I personally like it."

I just sat there and nodded. Spoken like medical personnel. I didn't understand any of it, but I didn't care. The bacon smoothie felt good, if it could keep me from, I hated the words—killing anyone.

Nadia's mouth pursed. "Ah, still squeamish. Well, that will pass eventually. Hey, I have an idea." She checked her watch and then flipped through her phone, texting someone. "You busy tonight?"

"Well," I considered. I had never been much for going out on a weekday, even if I wasn't going to work and school. As a philosophy student at Hunter College in my senior year, my classes are all about done. I only had my final project due the first week in May. My job kept me busy, and I liked to stay busy. So, what if sometimes work followed me home and stayed with me through my dreams? I needed the time to process the files and reorganize them, first into color based on year and then alphabetical. Mitch couldn't believe the library could keep me busy. He got bored just looking at the building.

Thursday was also my day to catch up on all my shows. The Upper East Side took its toll financially, even with my scholarship, student loans, and financial aid. I had to cancel my digital recorder until my economic prospects brighten. The financial aid only came every three months, and I used it on tuition. And I hated waiting until my shows were on the Internet. Though I had to admit, this was selfish of me to turn down Nadia for my foolish fascination with Natalie Dormer.

"Nothing. I'm not doing anything tonight," I said, reassuring myself.

"Great! I'll be back to pick you up at eleven."

"At night?" Sorry, it slipped out.

"Of course," she smirked at me. "Oh, right. I forget you aren't used to the schedule. It's when the club opens."

I couldn't hide how I felt. My principles were being thrown out the window, and I felt completely transparent.

"Hey," Nadia grabbed my shoulder reassuringly. "We'll go tomorrow. The shake will do you good. Just relax, and I'll call you later."

"Thanks," I muttered.

"By then, we'll have your new clothes and everything."

"I have new clothes?"

"There is a standard for vampires, you know. The Gap is not going to cut it."

"But I got a really good deal on this shirt."

She smiled serenely, enjoying watching me squirm in my skin. "Your Jersey roots are beginning to show. I want to introduce you to the New York Vampire lifestyle. You're one of the elites now. A quick pop into Old Navy isn't going to work on this crowd. Not like quickly buying a new shirt for a family reunion. Vampires around the world wish they were us. And we live in a fashion Mecca." She quickly put on her hooded cloak to leave. "I like you, Ollie, but you have no idea what your new world is like. Trust me on this."

I smiled nervously and waved goodbye. She was right though; I did need to trust her.

4

LETTING

"THE COMIC AND THE TRAGIC LIE INSEPARABLY
CLOSE, LIKE LIGHT AND SHADOW."

I stayed up very, very late, which was so uncharacteristic of me, but the protein from the pomegranate smoothie really helped my body change. I was too restless to sleep much anyway. I wasn't sure how to sleep anymore. The television helped my mind numb a little, and I forgot the newness of everything, bringing back the old me, if only for a moment.

I woke startled to the sound of gunfire. Mitch's shouting accompanied the violence from the video game.

"What are you doing here?" I asked, still shaking awake.

"My Playstation broke."

"Again?"

"Yeah," he mumbled, not blinking, and without losing concentration on his target. "I got cheese in it."

I scratched my head and rubbed the sleep from my eyes. I glanced at the clock; it was four in the afternoon. "Didn't that happen to your Xbox?"

He grumbled a yes.

"I still don't know how you get cheese in your machines."

"Chili Cheese Nachos. El Toro below my building has the yummiest. I just need to lick my fingers before I touch anything."

Mitch and I tried being roommates once. That cured me of living with anyone. It works best if he just visits.

I looked briefly at the plate next to him, the remains of a charbroiled steak ringed around in its own juice.

"Where did you get that?"

"Your freezer. It was fantastic. I usually don't look in there for anything but Freezies. It's been years since you had meat in your place. I couldn't resist."

I stuffed a pillow over my face and vented quick anger. "Please, don't touch my stuff." I said it, but I couldn't be too upset. It was like telling a dog not to eat the T-bone in his dish. I worried more that I might have steak and cheese in my gaming system.

I really needed to eat, so I went to the kitchen to follow one of Nadia's homemade recipes for curbing the blood-thirsty craving. This one was a little strange, blending coconut milk with lamb's stomach. The more I contemplated, the more convinced I became that Nadia had played a cruel joke, getting me to drink a haggis shake.

Mitch and I played video games together until the door buzzed. I looked at the clock. It was nine. Yikes! What happened to the day? It was Nadia and a friend. I buzzed her up and quickly shoved what I could in the couch and out of sight. I wished she had called first, but I'd forgive her. Mitch hardly moved as I worked around him.

"Hey, Ollie." Nadia greeted me with two small pecks, one on each cheek. She looked stunning, dressed all in black. "This is my friend Tivoli Holyoak."

Tivoli was thin and blonde with the darkest eyes I'd ever seen. Like Nadia, she was dressed very well, surely in the newest from some foreign runway. I glanced at her legs. I couldn't help myself. I hoped she didn't notice.

"Nice to meet you."

Her eyes intensified. "Yes, it is." She spoke with a slightly upturned smile.

I took her hand and tried the best I could to forget that she was *definitely* a vampire. My reaction to Tivoli—this girl was a man-eater. Never find yourself caught alone in a dark alley with her. She had, without any doubt in my mind, sucked life away from the living male population, probably several times.

Then I hesitated. What about Mitch? How would she react to my living best friend? My apartment was too small to hide him. I grabbed Nadia's arm and leaned in her ear. "How is she with—?" indicating with a shoulder shrug in Mitch's direction.

"We'll see," she whispered back and then winked. I don't think she worried about it, but I wasn't convinced.

"Hiyah, Mitch," I said trying to distract him from the game.

"Huh?" he grumbled and looked at me. He took a double take at the women who just entered the room.

"You remember Nadia from the clinic and—" I hesitated for the briefest second. "Uh, yes, this is Tivoli."

Mitch took one look and blinked; his attitude changed immediately. He stood up rather quickly and fingered through his hair.

"Hello ladies, I'm Mitch DiStefano." He didn't miss a step of his charm. That was one thing I never could figure out about Mitch, how women always found him irresistible. I could blame it on his helplessness or stupidity, which women fall for, apparently. He became a different person around girls, and they fell for it. He had the same charm in high school, and

I couldn't figure out how it worked. I had to admire it, like a superpower I would never have.

"Yes, I remember you from the clinic," Nadia replied with a raised eyebrow. "You couldn't stop laughing."

"Some things never change," Mitch returned.

Did he have to make fun of me in front of girls? But I laughed it off.

I could see Tivoli eying him critically, interested or perplexed, I couldn't tell. She might have even been impressed. After being around vampires for a while, you might find the living rather dull, I figured.

"I've brought some things for you," Nadia turned to me. She held two black paper sacks with an insignia that I didn't recognize—the mentioned Clothing she promised yesterday.

"What is VO?" I asked looking at the monogram.

"Vaughn Oldstrom."

"I've never heard of him."

"He's very exclusive and has a small shop here in New York. But that is the store's Living name. We know it as Vampires Only."

"He's a vampire?"

"I told you, Parker, there are a lot more here than you'd expect."

I thought Tivoli made a sincere smile at that remark.

Nadia pulled out a few sweaters made of soft, rich knit, two silk shirts of pale gray and blue, a black pull-over, and the most expensive jeans I'd ever seen.

"You have to return these," I remarked after seeing the price tag.

"Forget it," Nadia waved her hand absently. "I couldn't help myself. The new line is out. Vaughn insisted you have these. He donated them to the cause. He liked your story and took pity on you." There was a laugh stuck in her throat, and I don't know why, but I thought I was an inside joke of some sort.

I quickly stepped in the shower before I dressed in one of the silk shirts and the pair of expensive jeans, instantly liking the way the silk shirt fit. When I looked in the mirror, I stared dumbfounded. This wasn't me. I still had my ugly, black-rimmed glasses, but the clothes made me look like I was trying too hard. I was pale and sickly, not like the striking vampires in the novels at the check stands. I looked like I had a heart condition or some kidney disease. Maybe some gel in my hair might help. My first real night out as a vampire and I felt like a complete loser.

Mitch, meanwhile, was getting along fantastically with the girls. When I returned, he was entertaining them with one of our childhood stories. I felt embarrassed.

Nadia became distracted by my presence. "Hey, you look good. I guessed at the size, but they fit all right."

"I don't know," I said, moving around in the new clothes like a child.

"Well, let me fix something." Nadia ran her fingers in my hair, sculpturing peaks and spikes. "That should do. Not that you didn't look good before, Ollie, but I think this just might help. You coming, Mitch?"

I looked stunned for a moment. She was acting like this was normal. Was it? Mitch was *Living*. Was he even allowed to come? What if someone was really hungry? It didn't stop the girl who bit me. She had to be desperate.

Mitch changed his shirt and sharpened his hair. He was a good-looking guy and never looked too scruffy. His day growth on his beard attracted girls, not repelled them. I checked my baby face. Not one hair, typical. I guess I couldn't grow facial hair anymore, not that I ever could. I'd always wanted a soul patch to match my glasses. I guess I'd missed my opportunity.

I hadn't traveled outside my apartment since I visited Dr. Heck. Everything was the same, but different, like a room that once was painted blue had changed to red. The markets and shops with people working and customers shopping all looked the same, doing the same thing… but it was all different. These people were all ignorant to the idea of real vampires living among them. They just lived and breathed every day, going about their own business exactly like I had every day, willing to laugh at the very idea of vampires. However hard I imagined it wasn't real, my eyes would never shut again. I could never return to regular life, just like the movie the Matrix—I now knew the truth and I had to live it.

We headed Downtown. I found it strange that Nadia preferred to use the subway instead of a taxi to get there.

"The Underground are my kind of people," she said.

She was taking us to a club called The Cell. I had heard of the club before but had never dreamed of actually going. I was not a fan of crowds. People gave me anxiety. The place had a reputation as a hardcore industrial nightclub, electronic vibe and eclectic people, strobe lights and cage dancers. It never appealed to my mild taste.

On our stroll to Lexington Station, Nadia told me more about it. "The Cell means Blood Cell, not caged prison like many think. Sure, it has that also, but it's just to keep a dangerous image."

"It worked," I muttered. Even with the new life I lived, I still had fears, and I didn't want to go. I didn't know what I was getting into.

We traveled down to Chelsea, to an industrial park near the waterfront. The exterior spoke nothing special of the place, just a gray boxy building like many others. There were a few people hanging around a dark door who took interest in my company. We entered a long hallway. The industrial music blared loud behind the walls, muffled screams and thumping adding to the pockets of conversations coming from the interesting people waiting to get in. They glared at us as we walked past.

"Nadia!" a cry came from the front of the line. A tall man flagged her down.

"Ty!" she yelled back and waved. "Come," she whispered in my ear and grabbed my arm, knowing I would not go willingly. As we walked to the front of the line, I looked at everyone we passed who still waited. The looks could kill. I was worried about our safety immediately.

The man, Ty, was enormous, holding back the line of wannabes. There was no way he would let us in.

"Ty, this is Oliver and Mitch."

Ty nodded. "With you, huh? Round the back." This he motioned toward the lined curtains past the main entrance.

Nadia whispered something to him that I couldn't hear and then smiled back at me. "Nervous?"

"Nah," I played it off, trying as hard as I could to be totally comfortable with the idea. She saw through it. Her face brightened at my anxiety. She was enjoying this. I didn't know how to reply. What was she up to?

As we passed the entry, I glanced in. The Cell did not disappoint. It was just as I expected. Loud music, crowded, dancing in cages, colors bouncing off industrial steel—if my palms could sweat, they would have.

Behind the dark curtain wound a tight steel staircase. The whole time I kept thinking this was the strangest experience I've ever had. Where was she taking us? The top of the stairs opened to a balcony overlooking the entire dance floor. A railing went all the way around the club, and I could see everything—the lights, the crowd—the grandeur was overwhelming. I enjoyed the noise much better at this height. Nadia led us forward to a metal door. We entered and scaled another flight of stairs to a large room filled with talk.

A huge window looked over the main dance floor. The muffled sound of industrial music stimulated the more social atmosphere.

I felt like an initiate into a highly exclusive club or invited to an important people party by mistake. The partygoers all looked very expensive: boots, leather, diamonds, and silks— and here I was, out of place, like usual. I would have to thank Nadia later for the clothes.

Tivoli and Nadia excused themselves for a second to meet some friends and left Mitch and me to take in the scene.

"Good job," Mitch muttered to me.

"What do you mean?"

"Being a vampire has its privileges, to say the least. I've never been to the Executive Lounge."

"You talk like you've been here before."

"Of course I have." Mitch pushed me sideways. "Some of my DT buddies from work wanted to come last January. I met this Latvian girl named Ludja. I've never seen anyone so beautiful."

I loved how Mitch mentioned his job as if it were a real job with real money. DT stood for Day Trader but sitting around playing World of Warcraft all day wasn't a job. He started with me at Hunter four years ago, but that didn't last long—any excuse to move to New York. A year ago, he took out several micro-loans on the same day and started investing them in stocks. He will get up, trade and sell every few hours during the day while still in his pajamas and in-between games. I think it's so risky, I'm too sensible for a venture like that. I secretly hoped someday it caught up with him, but then, at what cost, I knew I would have to bail him out.

"Mitch, did you ever consider the girl you met might be one of these people?"

"Oh, come on," Mitch returned. "If she was a vampire, don't you think she would have sucked my blood?"

"Maybe," I answered, still not sure what to think about this place. "The more I learn, the weirder reality gets."

Nadia returned and introduced us to some of her friends. Every one of them had cool names: Jovanny, Cohl, Elcira, Amram, Krysztof—once you become a vampire, I figured you have to change your name to something mysterious and dark. Oliver Brixby wouldn't do for these people.

"Everyone, this is Oliver," Nadia introduced. Of course, I hadn't thought of a new name yet, so it's just as well.

"Meech! Meech!" a yell came from across the room; a tall brunette waved at my friend. This must be the girl Mitch had mentioned. She was indeed a vampire, and holy, she was beautiful. Everyone here was beautiful. I felt like placing a bag over my head.

"We're going to go dance, Nadi," Tivoli told her. She had her arm around Mitch. I think she wanted him away from Ludja. "You want to come?"

"Not yet," Nadia said.

"Hey, be careful with him," I told her. Tivoli's smile read mischief, but she nodded.

"Ollie, loosen up," Mitch said. "Have a drink or something." They left, Tivoli nearly dragging him away from the Latvian beauty.

I didn't mean to sound overly protective or paranoid when my best friend left to dance with a vampire I didn't trust. I just sounded stupid.

"Would you like a drink?" Nadia's voice broke my train of thought.

"A drink?" I still couldn't tell what she was up to. I guess this was my test. This was what I had been waiting for, the drink of life or whatever. "What is there, I mean, besides the obvious?"

She just smiled as she turned toward the bar. "I'll find something for you."

Then it was just me, standing by myself with these vampires with cool names staring at me. I didn't know what to say, so I just rocked on my heels.

"So, Oliver? Tell us about you?" the blond named Krysztof asked. His size was average, but his intimidating presence was enormous.

"About me?" I didn't like talking about me. I was the dullest person I knew. "I'm from New Jersey." The silence told me enough about what they thought. "I like, or liked being healthy or try, no tried to be healthy." I trailed off at that point. "Sorry, I guess that's boring. Umm . . . I like reading, I guess, if any of you like reading."

"What do you do, Oliver?" Krysztof asked again. "What is your employment?"

"Well, I'm a senior at Hunter College and I work at the Wexler Library as an archivist. It's nothing important really, but it's nice to have a campus job and keeps my mind active."

"Interesting."

"Really?" I wished I hadn't just blurted it out like that, it was anything but interesting.

"Student at Hunter?" Krysztof said thinking. "What are you studying? I had a cousin who taught Jewish Studies there."

"Philosophy… and Ancient Russian Culture I guess, if you like that kind of stuff."

The others in the circle showed collective interest Were they impressed or amused?

"Philosophy? I don't think I have ever had a philosopher." Krysztof looked at those around. "This should be interesting. Don't you think?"

Small audible laughs came out of their mouths. I laughed along too. "So, what should be interesting?"

"Your management," he returned, sipping a little from wine glass and smiling.

What did he mean by that? I still smiled insecurely. "I'm sorry. I don't think I understand what you mean by management."

Krysztof lifted the corner of his mouth questioning.

"I think you misunderstood him," another man named Cohl jumped in. "Krysztof is more like our Human Resource Manager, but for non-humans. He finds us jobs, gets us careers."

"I'm not following."

"It's not easy to be what we are." The exquisite Elcira joined in the conversation. "Krysztof helps place us in an acceptable environment."

"Like Nadia," Krysztof pointed out. "She was in the Army when she was bitten. I had a scout in Houston who witnessed what had happened to her and placed her in quarantine. He sent her to Bronx VA where we first met. She had a medical background in the Army, so I set her up with Dr. Leonard

Heckenliable, a good friend of mine, who has helped us out many times. Nadia has been there for two years, I believe."

Reality again altered before my eyes. I never considered this side of the vampire world. Vampires didn't need jobs. They would invite rich women to their big castles and drink them and live off their money. I mean, I figured that was how vampires lived, right?

Then I recalled the girl, that desperate, sickening girl that bit me in the park, and I felt pity for her. Here I was in vampire luxury, probably about to drink imported blood or something, and she was so starving, enough to want a taste of me. I remembered how she spit up my blood. A stupid idea, tasting me. Anyone else might taste sweet, but me? Ick!

"So, how has Krysztof helped you?"

Elcira, the rather ethereal red-headed beauty—if I could use the word—spoke up. "I was a dancer at ABA. My attacker left me for dead. At first, I didn't know what was wrong with me. I tried to return to normal life but was so sick and weak I thought I might die, but I never did. I had gone mad. I wandered around the city like a zombie. I remember curling up, ready for death, and it never came. Krysztof has sources, I don't know how, but he knew of the attack. He searched for me and found me deep in a back alley in Brooklyn and explained everything. He helped me learn how to get my body back into a dancing, physical condition, which is not easy, considering my body had altered after the change. But now, I teach dance classes at night and have worked on Broadway. It was a true miracle that he found me."

"Seriously? You didn't know what happened to you?"

Her eyes connected with mine. "Who was going to explain it to me?" she answered. "Did you? Would you have believed it if someone told you, you are now a vampire?"

Good point. She hit it right on the head. I'm still fighting the idea. "Yeah. Sorry. I think I understand you now."

"Teaching dance allows me to work at night and freedom to live the right lifestyle for me."

"And what about you?" I asked the other two men, standing by Krysztof, the ones named Cohl and Jovanny.

"I'm in music," Cohl answered, a sharp-dressed man in a bright red suit. "I'm a record producer with Cutthroat Records. Do you know it?"

I shook my head, but I really had never been one for hip hop music.

Jovanny smiled a big toothy grin. He was a character; I could tell from his casual attitude and more casual manner of dress. His ringer t-shirt read *Look at Me Still Talking When There's Science to Do.* "I do online gaming worlds and LARP in the park. I create computer viruses on the side."

Interesting. "What is LARP?" I had to ask.

"Live Action Role Playing," he answered as if everyone should know. "There are others of us that play."

The dangers of Central Park just elevated. Was it enough to have freakishly tiny girls biting the first person they see but knowing there were vampires actually acting out as wizards, using real weapons and everything, frankly, made me nervous.

"Here you go," Nadia returned with a drink. "I'm playing it safe and got you a Bloody Mary."

"Very funny," I laughed with them. The smell of the drink filled my senses and brought images to my brain; memories of hospital waiting rooms and freshly stitched wounds. How strange the memories sparked from the smell?

"Where did you get the…?" I trailed off.

"The blood is donated here at the club," Cohl remarked. "We have what we call the Letting Room below us. Once guests get too intoxicated, we send them to our suites in the back where we draw about a pint or so from them for our storage. They don't remember anything afterwards. Have you ever donated?"

"Eck, no." My response came out faster than my brain wished.

Cohl took in the comment, but then continued. "Well, the removal of blood can be wearing on the body, so they think it's only from the partying the night before, easily enough like a hangover. It also works for us because of whatever alcohol might be in their blood."

Again, my brain started acting human. "But don't you worry where the blood came from? What kind of disease might be in their blood?"

"What do we care?" Jovanny answered. "What kind of damage is it going to do to us?"

I guess it did seem silly for me to worry about such a thing. I can't really die again, can I? "Well said. Okay, then." I tried the drink.

I slowly took a sip. The human blood tingled my tongue and sent my senses dancing. The sensation felt weird in my mouth and down my throat. My body warmed and gently tingled around my extremities. The heat increased to a fire as it spread around my body very quickly and then to my head. Instantly there was a throbbing, pounding in my temples. Was this typical for this drink? Then my vision blurred and disappeared.

I hit the floor, and my body began to shake. I remembered throwing up a little before I completely passed out.

5

THE DAMAGE OF SULFA

"A SYSTEM OF MORALITY WHICH IS BASED ON RELATIVE EMOTIONAL VALUES IS A MERE ILLUSION, A THOROUGHLY VULGAR CONCEPTION WHICH HAS NOTHING SOUND IN IT AND NOTHING TRUE."

I woke on a circular bed with a silky blanket over me. The room was dimly lit with bubbled sconces among the red drapery. If I had ever conceived entering a vampire lair, this room would fulfill my imagination. I concentrated on the little details in the mahogany molding and marble-carved statues until I felt too disoriented. I lay back on the pillows.

Voices came from just outside the room. I couldn't really make out anything that was said, and I didn't really care. I just let my mind think, like it always had when I woke mid-sleep and couldn't get back to bed.

Then I heard my name. I moved soundlessly on the sheets closer to the voices. They were male voices I didn't know well enough to distinguish.

"…and I think you are over-reacting."

"…I think Lennox is our only hope here."

"But if it's the blood, how will he help?"

"Lennox is an expert at this. My skills only cover probabilities until evidence is found."

"And maybe it's not the blood. Maybe it was whatever the person drank that affected him—"

"Nadia is checking on that—"

"…but I'm more concerned about his condition now."

"Nice theory, Krys, but what does it really matter to us anyway. We hardly know this guy."

"If Nadia means anything to you, Jo, you might care."

"I don't like what you're implying there, Andrus."

There was silence. I tried to move closer, but the silk sheet rubbed on my jeans and caused a *swip* of fabric on fabric. I tried being quiet as I leaned my head closer, hanging off the bed. Within two seconds my entire body slipped off the bed and thumped on the floor.

The curtain opened and three men looked down on me: Krysztof, Jovanny, and another I did not know. They all looked puzzled at my crumbled heap. Jovanny leant his hand to help me up.

"You doing okay?" he asked as I staggered back to my feet.

"Lie back down, would you please?" Krysztof asked. "I don't want to be held accountable for disobeying orders."

"From who?" I asked, sitting back on the bed.

"From Nadia, of course," Jovanny entered. "She can become quite insistent."

I understood, but honestly, my head was still swimming. "Where am I?"

"This is my personal room," Krysztof answered. "We are behind the Executive Suite. I use it for my own personal entertaining."

I shut my ears at the idea.

"What happened to me back there?"

"We don't know," Jovanny answered. "Nadia thought you might be poisoned. Or maybe you're just a wuss."

I ignored the comment. "Poisoned? That doesn't make any sense."

"That's why I like my theory."

"But if I am a vampire, I should be immune to this, right?"

"You would think so."

I couldn't tell if Jovanny was just being sarcastic or blatantly rude. I just sighed it away and figured I was the problem here.

"We asked Andrus to help us here," Krysztof introduced the dark, bearded Andrus who gave me hope for facial hair. He reminded me of Blade—the Vampire Hunter—he looked that cool. I immediately liked him. "Andrus is a doctor."

Andrus moved to the bed and quickly did an assessment of me. He didn't make any tell-tale sounds of my condition. I thought my days with doctors were over.

"Are you a doctor of the living or the Undead?" I asked while he examined my throat.

"Well," he answered in a deep boom, "I have only need of seeing the living. You would be the first among us I have seen for any medical reason. I've never heard of a vampire passing out."

I decided I should be honest with my health care professional. "I've never handled alcohol very well. Does that matter?"

"No," he laughed. "The alcohol has very little effect on our bodies, not as much as others might think or hope it does."

Jovanny's face fell a little at that. "No, this has to do with something else, and I don't know what it might be. We were discussing a probability of medications the person whom it came from was on, or maybe the different flavors that were put in the drink. I know Nadia likes to experiment with flavors. Can you tell me what you were allergic to in human state?"

It might be easier to start with what I was not allergic to, but I started listing different grasses, nuts, dogs, cats, well, animals, and certain fruits.

"You were allergic to strawberries," Jovanny uttered. "How did you survive?"

The question was facetious, but I answered it anyway. "I'm very careful about what I put in my body, or was, you know, just in case. I mean, I am… or was—tried to be a vegetarian."

All three vampires made an "Ewe" sound.

"Maybe that has something to do with it?" Krysztof asked Andrus positively.

"No. Nadia said she made him a shake the other day using meat, so it's not the enzymes he can't handle."

"I don't understand what you're talking about," I interrupted. "You need to explain."

"There is something wrong with your vampire blood," Krysztof answered.

"It's more like your vampire body," Andrus corrected. "It doesn't have the same stability as the rest of us."

"I don't…" the words fell out of my mouth.

"Your body hasn't much changed since you were attacked, right?"

"I guess, but what was I to expect?"

Andrus saw my panic and answered. "Your body should've entered through a molecular change, strengthening the organs and stomach for your new food source. Your muscles become firmer, fit for better tolerance and resilience. But look at you."

I didn't like that they all looked at me as a skinny vampire reject. "So, I'm not a vampire."

"I wouldn't say that." Jovanny entered. "But you seem to be allergic to blood."

I sank my head back on the bed. The others thought I passed out again.

Krysztof turned to Andrus. "If I notify Lennox tonight, he might have something by Wednesday."

"Wednesday?" I said with my head still on the bed. I tried my best to sound indignant, but it cracked at the end, like a teenage boy. Honestly, I didn't know what I was indignant about at this point. I didn't know anything anymore.

"It takes time to set up donors," Andrus answered. Still no help.

"Well, what am I going to do until then? What about work and school?"

"School?" Jovanny asked. "You still going to do that?"

"I have responsibilities," I answered as I sat up again. "I mean, I don't know anything else," and it hit me. "What am I going to tell my parents?" Why hadn't I considered them— Bill and Shirley Brixby of humble Lakeshore, New Jersey. The proud expectations of their only child came crashing down around me. The others were laughing. I think it must be a common problem. "Do you have a pamphlet for that too?" I asked stupidly.

"Nadia will take care of you," Krysztof assured me.

"Where's Mitch?" My thinking of my family came around to my friend.

"I'm not sure anymore," Krysztof turned to Jovanny. "Is he still hooked up?"

"He shouldn't be. He was a fast bleed. He's probably back with the girls."

"You took Mitch's blood?"

"Yes, but he volunteered," Krysztof clarified. "Said if he could help you, he would."

"Huh," escaped my lips. Mitch had always been selfish in my mind. This was new. I quickly questioned what he might be getting in return for this selfless act of service.

"Let's return you home," Krysztof said, lifting me to my feet. "I'll contact your work tomorrow and try to set you on your way. Just rest until we can figure this out."

I didn't care at the moment, but home sounded like the best option, like normalcy. My sleep schedule was changing, but I still felt dizzy and drained from the drink. Jovanny found Mitch, still laughing and enjoying the company of both Tivoli and Ludja. He left the tempting vampires and graciously took me home.

6

NORMALCY

"THE WAY TO GAIN A GOOD REPUTATION IS
TO ENDEAVOR TO BE WHAT YOU DESIRE TO
APPEAR."

I hid in my apartment for the rest of the weekend. I tried to get some reading in, but my classic reads taste couldn't subdue my psychological state. In every novel I picked up, after the first chapter, I envisioned the main character being chased by undead vampires. I don't think John Steinbeck planned it that way. After the defeating tries to keep my brain occupied, I finally turned on Mitch's video game and started a new character.

Come Monday, I needed to return to school and to work. School wouldn't be a problem, with only weeks left in my bachelors. Most of my class work I could finish online. I had a pretty good rapport with my professors. I might have to step out in the sun to take an exam or two, or turn in some papers, but for being my last semester of school I felt confident. I think that grad school might be put off for a little while until I figure everything out.

Work I couldn't miss anymore. I needed the money, and my conscience was eating at me. But Krysztof seemed a good person to have around and somehow got Warren, my boss, to get me a later shift. I could even work after the library closed. I felt lucky to even have a job at this point.

Nadia set me up with some more exotic recipes, and Mitch agreed to go shopping for me as long as he got to eat some steaks with me. The shakes were okay, but the taste was starting to dull. It wasn't enough. Dr. Andrus was confident this Lennox could help. They sent some more samples to him for a better diagnosis in upstate New York and come Wednesday, Andrus, Nadia, and I planned a trip there that evening.

Sunday night Nadia called and asked me to meet her in the fashion district. Mitch, for once, wasn't there. He went out Saturday with some of his DT buddies and got smashed. He wouldn't resurface for a few days.

I left from Lexington Ave to Penn Station at a quarter to nine. I hadn't been down that direction for a while. I remembered coming to New York four years ago, excited to see the sites when I was a young freshman, thinking the city was the most amazing place in the world. I had a lot more energy then. Now it was hard to get up in the morning and be motivated about anything. I began feeling more and more depressed the longer I stayed in New York. Mitch blamed my major—made me think too much. I really needed my Pamelor.

Nadia was there waiting for me as I stepped off. It still seemed pretty crowded for a Sunday night.

"There's a basketball game tonight," Nadia explained. "Come on." She wrapped her arm around mine, and we strolled down a few blocks. I became rather chatty.

"So, are you going to tell me about how you turned into a vampire?"

Nadia smiled. "Can you guess?"

I could guess forever and never get it right. "Is it true you were in the Army?"

Nadia stopped. "How did you know that?"

I had to confess. "Krysztof mentioned something like that."

"Figures he'd tell you." She grimaced. "It's not very interesting. People assume it must be interesting when you turn into something so glamorous, but sorry."

"Have you killed anyone?" I couldn't help myself. I was curious.

"Oh, sure…" she trailed off. My look of uncom-fortable shock wasn't disguised very well. "Ollie, come on. Man up. You are a Vamp now. Sorry if you don't like it, but there is no way to change it. If you care to know about the people, don't. It was humane. Though I don't like the taste of old people, it's easy to drain them completely. If you don't drain them, they come back. The bigger the person, the sweeter the blood—the fat and sugars floats in the veins," she made a yummy sound. "There is something about the taste of Twinkies in the blood stream."

I started to gag.

"But mostly," she continued, "I stick with my smoothies and extractions. I like to live a healthier lifestyle than some of the others."

We passed a giant button.

"Where are you taking me?" I suddenly considered.

"I want you to meet Vaughn, my fashion friend, remember?"

"The guy who gave me the clothes?"

"He's going to set us up."

"Nadia, I don't have the money for this," the confession was a little timid. Every time I've seen her, she's looked dynamite.

"I don't want you to think about it right now," she assured me.

We turned the corner to a very old-looking gray building with an old-fashioned door and archway. Nadia took a key from out of her purse and unlocked it.

"You have a key?"

Nadia grinned a little. "I come here a lot," she admitted.

Inside was a small shop that looked closed for the day. Tee shirts and jeans lines the dark walls. It was quiet, except for Nadia's boots echoing on the hard floors. We moved past the racks to another door in the back. There was a small intercom placed on the wall.

…Buzz…

"It's me."

A click unlocked the door, and we stepped into a long white hallway. I just followed Nadia's clomping down to a pair of double doors. The atmosphere felt so strange to me, like I was entering a version of the Matrix.

Nadia smirked a little as she reached the door. "Ready, Parker?"

I shrugged. I guess I didn't care.

She opened the door, and I had to blink a few times to make sure my pupils were focusing right. Inside was a grand room decorated by Bram Stoker himself. It felt like I was walking onto a Hollywood movie set. The walls were dark with long, red velvet curtains lining the majestic nightlife of the city. There were dim chandeliers and flickering candlelight on the ceiling and long, antique furniture filling the room with rich fabrics.

"'Ello 'ello 'ello," came from around the corner.

A man about half the size of me came out of nowhere to greet us. He had fun, white tuffs of hair on each side of his head, and his grin brightened the entire area.

Nadia greeted him with some language they both spoke, and I didn't and kissed him on each cheek.

"Vaughn, this is Oliver Brixby. Ollie, this is Vaughn Ohlstrom."

"Willkommen," he held out his hand in greeting.

"Love the place," I said without anything else to say. "Are you from Transylvania?"

He smiled with a little humph.

"Vaughn is from Germany," Nadia entered. "But he loves the idea of Transylvania, don't you?"

"Ah, yes," he said in his sweet accent. "I love, love Europe romance. Sweet to my heart." He padded his chest a little. "Come my Nadalina, I have some-ting new."

He moved us into a different room. It looked fairly the same, but brighter, and there were long tables with different sewing machines placed about. On one side there were racks of ornate clothes all hung in different stages of construction. Vaughn guided us to a mannequin wearing a long black silhouetted dress with unique black buttons down the side.

"For you, my dear," he said.

"It's ready?" Nadia stated in surprise. She went and fussed over the stitches and stuff I couldn't see or had any clue about. "You like it, Ollie?"

A weird question. "Sure, I guess. What's it for?"

"I'm going to a big event at the end of the month. Big VO Gala."

"A date?" It was a stupid thing to say. And I don't know how it slipped out of my mouth. She can date whoever she wanted. I had spent a few long hours with her, but I had no right to pry about her personal life. "Yeah, umm. Sounds like fun."

Nadia looked at me with a slight nervous grin and then continued to examine it.

I took a moment to inspect his workspace. I stupidly placed my hand down on one of the workspaces and poked myself with a needle. It still hurt, but not as I expected it to—more like tingling pressure than a poke. I squeezed it a few times just to make sure I wasn't making it up, but there was no blood.

"Here, sir, come," Vaughn hailed me over to a rack of clothes. "Now, I have right here my VO essentials—a starter kit for new vampires like you."

"A starter kit?" I was impressed. I really did luck out with meeting Nadia, didn't I?

"Yes, yes," he continued in his funny excited way. "Here is stretch jacket for day. Feel the material, nice and soft, UV protected material, but I make it real nice."

I touched the fabric. Felt like any other material you might wear skiing, I imagined. Honestly, if Vaughn was looking for encouragement from me about his fashion, I was the last person to ask. If I could hide under a sweatshirt every day of my life, I would.

"Look at the glasses. Look!" He handed me some very nice, very expensive sunglasses. "Special protectant. Look!"

"Are they prescription?" I took off my black frames and casually I put on the new ones. Everything in the room changed colors. "Whoa," escaped. Now I really felt like I was in the Matrix. "How did you do that?"

"Heat sensitive."

I looked at Nadia. The aura around her looked bluish, like some lovely fairy light I'd always imagined elves had back in my RPG days. "So, this picks up heat from people."

"Yes, but it also helps you identify who is not."

"Gotcha." I couldn't wait to try these out. I looked down at the little man and saw a red heat coming from him. "Wait. You're human?"

"Yes," Nadia entered. "So, treat him really well, Parker."

I stared confused, but passed it by, like everything else I had to get used to.

Vaughn spread out other things, such as sunscreens, toothbrushes, mouthwash, all made for vampires. "This first free. Second… not so free." He laughed to himself. It felt like he was my personal drug dealer.

I looked over the jeans, sweaters, shirts, there were so many. "All this?"

"Yes," he said. "You need this. And you can't find it out there. I try to help out my poor friends, and in return they help me."

Nadia smiled wide at the man. "Yes and thank you for this. Can I try it on?"

Vaughn agreed and sent her behind a screen to change. When she returned, my jaw dropped. I was apologizing right now for what I was thinking at that moment. I've never seen anything fit so perfect. Her hips, her curves—she could eat any man in that, no doubt. "Do all… sorry, all vampire girls, I mean, look like you?"

Her head cocked to the side. "Nope," she uttered popping the "P" at the end. I cleared my throat. Nadia knew she had my attention.

I avoided the awkwardness I felt and focused on my new stuff. Vaughn placed my clothing in paper bags with the intricate VO insignia. Even the bag looked expensive. Even if this stuff was free, I would need more eventually, and that was not going to be cheap.

The price of the vampire lifestyle would not be cheap.

I have always been a clean guy, never one to miss my roll of showering the manly stink away. I'm not a fan of being dirty or dirt or bugs crawling on my skin. And I'm man enough to admit I used Axe body wash a few times, honestly thinking it would attract girls, like in the commercials. But all these new products left me baffled. In the bag I found scratchy soap, not soft to the touch, for the super delicate needs of the vampire skin, creams that smells like gerbil cages, weird colors, oils, dark purple shampoo that stained my shower wall, and a strange clear gel I had no idea what to do with.

I considered for a small second to ask Nadia but didn't want to go there. This shouldn't be hard. I had taken care of myself for years. It was embarrassing enough being the only vampire in history who couldn't drink blood.

But I dressed myself just fine on Monday, ready for my first day back at work. I felt nervous while I traveled down to campus. I had my hood up, even though it was overcast, which I have to admit, made me feel cooler than ever. The world turned blue in my new sunglasses, and I could see the reddish aura around all the people I passed. I felt like I could almost feel their pulse of life circulating their vulnerable human bodies. It was fascinating.

I entered the Wexler Library and headed up to the second floor, trying to play it as normal as I could.

"Whoa, Oliver, you look awful," Deborah said from behind the Reserve desk as I went back behind the counter to log on to the computer. She was a sweet, old thing who loved books and cats and knitting. "Did you really get—" she mouthed "Swine Flu" under her breath.

"Oh, yeah," I exaggerated. "And it's just as bad as everyone says."

"I knew it," she said. "Did you eat too much bacon?"

"Deborah, he's a vegetarian," Beth walked up to the counter. I always liked Beth—a music major in orchestra. I didn't remember what she played, but I knew she was really good. "Nice to see you out and about again."

"Thanks."

"Are you still contagious?" Deborah asked.

"Ah… No. I don't think so."

"Good. I got Curly Fries at home and don't want him getting all sick."

I looked at Beth for an explanation and she mouthed "new cat" to me. Deborah went through cats. I thought at first, she must have dozens of them around, but actually they just kept dying. It might be that they died from too much love, but I have my own theory—the cats committed suicide.

"What happened to McNugget?" I asked, trying to sound concerned.

"I'm not really sure. He wasn't eating enough, so I fed him mashed potatoes."

I speculated where the mashed potatoes came from or if they were mashed potatoes at all.

"I'm going to get a coffee," Beth said. "Want to join me?" This was Beth's queue to me she wanted to talk.

"Better not," I replied. She might think it odd for me to turn down our coffee time together, but I hadn't touched it since, well, you know. My mind drifted to my morning macchiato. My heart almost snapped at the thought. Maybe Nadia knew any coffee blend safe for our condition.

"You must not be feeling well."

"Not quite myself," I answered dryly. It was as truthful as I could be. When would I ever be myself?

I clocked in on the computer and looked through my pending emails. Yikes! There were a lot. I had one hundred and forty unread messages. I turned and looked at my basket. There was a huge stack of unprocessed paperwork all for me. I skipped the emails and headed to my desk to get to work. Work would get my mind off of everything else. Right?

"Brixby!" I heard loud and clear, surprised to hear something so loud in a library. Warren, my slob of a boss, looked dead in my eyes as he headed my direction. From the corner of my eye, Deborah busied herself with paper shuffling.

"Well, well, the zombie returns."

I should have thanked him for the zombie reference but thought better of it. "Hey," was all that came out.

He reached the counter and drummed his hairy knuckles in an agitated fashion. "Glad to have you back."

"Um… thanks."

"I have some papers for you to fill out." He handed over the yellow and pink sheets. "I don't like being made a fool." He shouldn't have started the sentence that way. As far as I saw him, the stained white shirt, the suspenders, the overly large glasses on his massive face—apparently, he does like being made a fool." If you are not coming to work, you need to contact someone directly. Because of it, here is a Leave of

Absence form, along with the Short Notice Absence form. I need you to fill out the medial discharge report and have your doctor sign it."

I stared at the documents with a blank expression.

"Also, I don't like being bullied," Warren added. I looked at him with confusion. He lowered his voice toward me. "Your friends, whoever they are, have no right to threaten me concerning my job and position. You may be Summa Cum Laud, but that doesn't mean you are not replaceable. If you are looking for a recommendation from me for grad school, forget it, and tell your friends to not contact me again."

I was taken back. It took me a second to process what on earth he was referring to, but it could only mean that the talk with Krysztof did not go as well as I thought. And I was not an angry person, it was not in my nature to be so, others knew that. I tended to get pushed around a bit. But, for the first time as a vampire, I thought I felt anger. This was not merely something that would fly by, I felt a pulsing, heated anger I always feared about vampires.

I looked directly in his eyes, and I think he could sense it.

"I expect those to be on my desk by Wednesday," he sputtered out as he walked away.

I looked at his mass and remembered what Nadia had told me about the fat ones tasting the best and thought I might take her up on it.

7

A DOWNWARD SPIRAL

"THEY ARE NOT ONLY IDLE WHO DO
NOTHING, BUT THEY ARE IDLE ALSO WHO
MIGHT BE BETTER EMPLOYED."

My strength was fading, I could tell, or maybe my will was waning. Whatever it was, my depression was sinking me, like a drowning cat reaching for air. I hadn't felt this low since my freshman year in high school when I asked Brenda Barfuss to dance, and she outwardly laughed at me and was so embarrassed she told the entire school I had a contagious rash. I became numb and void of all feeling. Ninth grade, my first experience with depression—after that I became much more introverted. Though I couldn't rain fire of revenge on her, since it just wasn't in my nature to do so, I figured she would have her own problems living with the last name Barfuss.

Work the next day was no better. I did join Beth for a coffee, but just kind of played with it. I had always been a good listener, and she liked to talk about her problems, whatever they were. I was a good listener, and a lousy adviser, but today I felt like neither.

"Ollie, are you okay?" Beth asked. "You haven't touched your coffee."

"I know," I replied without any idea what my next words would be.

"Do you want to talk about it? I can tell something's different about you."

"Really? Is it obvious?"

"You look like you need to eat, or sleep. Maybe we should get you some lunch."

"Good idea," I slipped. I was hungry. I was starving, to be honest.

"Do you want my carrot salad?" Bless Beth for being as vegan as I was.

"No," I sighed. I might break the news to her. "Thanks, Beth, but I think I can't be a vegetarian anymore."

Beth was stunned. "Don't say that, Ollie. You are the best person I know. You have always been committed to whatever you set your mind to. Look at you, getting up so early to run in the morning. Your humanitarian efforts, devoting your time to the Kid's Center, inspired me to volunteer."

She was wrong. That wasn't me. I wasn't that person anymore.

"Have you stopped taking your medications?"

She hit it right on the head, and I slumped a little in my chair.

"Ollie, you can't do that. Your body depends on those—"

"Sorry. Can you not lecture me on what my body needs? Thanks." I couldn't believe I was getting upset. She complimented me, and here I felt completely rude. I thought it best if I just got up and walk away.

Beth left me alone after that.

I slumped home around midnight to find Mitch back playing video games again. I was glad to see him actually. I was glad to have a friend again and having him around made me feel like me again.

I thought I made a mistake though. I mentioned my depression to Mitch.

"Didn't Nadia give you a card for that?"

"Huh?"

"I think there was a card for a vampire shrink," Mitch mentioned while he waited for the screen to load.

"You trying to help me?" I said a little sarcastically. I was a little hard to believe coming from him. It might have been a joke. I admitted that sometimes I didn't understand Mitch's sense of humor.

"I'm serious, Ollie," he continued, pausing the game as he turned toward me. "I met some fantastic vampires the other night, and they seemed happy."

"Yes, but they can drink blood."

"Are you telling me you would be happier if you could drink blood? Yeah, right. That's not the Oliver I know."

"Yeah, well, I don't know what happened to that fun-loving guy, but he lost his sense a humor when he passed out in front of the Vampire Elite." And here I was getting upset again. I crumpled to the ground and placed a pillow over my face.

"Oh, yeah, that reminds me," Mitch said as cool as ever. He reached over with one arm playing his game and grabbed a note from the couch. "Nadia's coming around nine tomorrow night. She said to dress nice, and I think she said there is something wrong with your blood too."

"Really?" I acted as if this was good news.

"Yeah, you should call her."

"At midnight?" I forgot the hours of a vampire.

Mitch shrugged a yes. And that is what I did. Within seconds I had Nadia on the phone.

"I was right," she said with a hollow echo, like she was standing in a bathroom stall. "There is something wrong with your blood."

"Yes!" I'd never been so excited about there being a problem. Problems I can handle. Problems were normal for me.

That is all she knew, but hopeful for more information tomorrow.

The news cheered me up so much, I made a bacon smoothie to celebrate.

The next day was long. I was anxious all day. By the time nine came around, I was a frantic wreck. Nadia arrived in a taxi, Dr. Andrus with her.

Mitch was ready to hop in also when Andrus stopped him. "Sorry, Mitch. This is no place for you."

"I think Oliver needs me there."

"Mitch," Nadia entered. "You don't want to go where we're going. This is not a place for someone like you. Do you get that?"

Mitch nodded, but I could see he was disappointed. Something crazy like this would be right up his alley.

"Where to?" the cabby asked as soon as we shut the door.

"Westchester, please," Nadia explained.

"Westchester? Where's that?" I asked, being stupid about the state I lived in. I knew my way through Jersey, but I never ventured much outside of Manhattan.

"North about an hour or so, depending on traffic. Lennox works at a small community hospital in Sleepy Hollow."

"Sleepy Hollow? Like the Washington Irving story?" I loved imaginative, historic fiction, like Poe, Twain, or Irving. This made things interesting. Did this vampire go around as the Headless Horseman? I knew the idea might be disturbing but amusing. I snickered to myself. Nadia looked at me just smiling, and then I felt stupid, grinning for no reason.

On our way, Andrus explained what they detected on my slides. I wish I understood more about medicine because a lot of it went over my head. I think he tried to make it confusing just in case the cabby listened in.

"Basically," he dumbed it down, "the chemicals already in your body prevented the VHN virus to penetrates deep in your marrow, causing the cellular chemical change. It stopped the growth of the virus and rejected the engrafting of the bacteria, in effect creating something like an antidote."

"Wait. What?" I caught the antidote part. "Are you saying I can be cured of this? That I can reverse this?"

"No," Andrus corrected. "It's not that simple. Your body had been in this state much too long to just suddenly wake up."

"But it can be done."

Nadia turned to hushed tones. "Listen, Parker, it isn't that easy. Lennox is our hope here, but this gets tricky. We don't know what this might do to you. It might help you or might harm you."

"But what could be worse than what I am now?"

"You could be a zombie," Andrus smoothed over.

Nadia smiled a crooked smile at the joke. "Lennox is a healthy living, someone like us, with very carnal hungers. His lifestyle is nothing that you've seen before. Even we don't like to meet with him."

My stomach dropped. "Then what is your plan?"

"We need to clear your body of the substance, whatever it was," Andrus said.

"How do we do that?"

"Through a red cell apheresis exchange."

I had donated plasma before, once. I had lived the life of a starving college student desperate for cash. I also remembered passing out shortly after donating.

"We'll hook you to the machine and hopefully change out whatever is in your blood stream with fresh new blood."

"From where?" I said a little creeped out.

"Lennox works in the blood bank. The blood is clean, I promise."

I liked the thought of blood being tested before tasted.

"He's agreed to do it," Andrus continued. "But there is a catch."

"What catch?"

They looked at each other, and they didn't need to answer. If this Lennox was as vampiristic as they said, nothing would satisfy except fresh blood.

"Krysztof has already arranged it."

"No way," I muttered. "I can't do this, if some girl has to die."

Nadia snapped her fingers right in my face. "Remember, man up. We can't help what we are."

"Sorry," I said. This was hard to take. I imagined a poor little lamb going for the slaughter of a horrible beast. The image of that poor girl who bit me popped back in my head—

someone as innocent as she is going to be made into someone's dinner...

... and I nearly passed out again.

$$8$$

THE DEAD MAN UNDER THE SHEET

"I ONLY WISH THAT ORDINARY PEOPLE HAD AN UNLIMITED CAPACITY FOR DOING HARM; THEN THEY MIGHT HAVE AN UNLIMITED POWER FOR DOING GOOD."

Sleepy Hollow was in every way as charming and as creepy as I fantasized. My nausea faded as we exited the highway. I was sure it would be nice during the day, but the old cemetery and stone architecture felt as cold to me as my own heart was now.

We wound around streets and up winding hills to get to the hospital. It was out of character compared to the charming town; it was a hospital, small and out-of-date, like so many I had visited before.

Nadia handed me a badge and a white coat. "Don't worry. No one is going to stop us. Andrus is a doctor, remember."

I hated this plan. I was the world's worst actor. Just ask my sophomore drama coach. She told me I was upstaged by the chair.

The three of us got out of the taxi and left to enter the hospital's right wing.

The door had a locked entry. Andrus just held up his badge and it turned green, allowing access. As we entered the hospital, security stood up on our left. It was late for visiting hours.

"Good evening, Dr. Brown," the security guard smiled. "Late to be here tonight."

"Yes," Andrus answered. "But Autopsy has a hard case tonight, and I've asked my two medical students to help with the matter."

"Very well. Just sign in."

There was a clipboard. I waited to see what Nadia wrote down, but she used her real name, so I did too.

We traveled down a hallway before we took a left into a different area. The hospital must have had additions added to it, because where we were heading looked nothing like the entrance. It was old, stark white like the psychiatric hospital in "One Flew Over the Cuckoo's Nest." We headed down a small set of stairs that led to another scary hallway. I read the signs pointing Blood Bank this way. Oddly enough, it was the same direction as Autopsy too.

There was a window at the Blood Bank, and Andrus rang a little bell. A smallish young woman in a white lab coat, fronting sharp red glasses, came to greet us.

"Hi. What do ya need?"

"Yes, we are looking for Dr. Lennox."

"I think he's in his office right around the corner. Probably knock before entering."

"Thanks," Andrus returned. I smiled my best at the girl, but she didn't seem interested and just went back to work.

We walked around the corner to a door that read 'Dr. Albert Lennox, Pathologist' and knocked.

"Come!" a shout echoed from the other side.

Andrus opened the door, and we walked into a very ordinary office filled with books and computers and instruments and other things. Right in the middle of the room was a long, skinny table with a white sheet draped over what I swore was a body. We had walked right into an autopsy, and I panicked. That was the last thing I wanted to see.

"Andrus, my good man," a voice came from somewhere in the room. I looked around but couldn't see anyone.

Just like out of a horror film the body under the sheet sat up. I gasped. I couldn't help it. It just slipped out. The sheet dropped and the face of a man resembling Dracula looked at me.

"Is this *he*?" he sneered in a deep voice.

Andrus walked up. I could sense he wasn't as confident about this either. "Good to see you again," he started. "Yes, this is Oliver Brixby."

"Hmmm," he sneered. "I needed to take a quick nap. The graveyard shift can be murder." He smirked a quirky smile at me—an oily, creepy smile. I couldn't tell if he was serious, so I smiled uncomfortably back. "Ah, but Nadia. It is always lovely to see you." He got up off the gurney and moved to take her hand. "As I have mentioned before, I wished it had been me that took your life."

"Thanks," Nadia said with a smirk.

"So... Oliver," he spilled my name out like venom from his tongue. "I have looked over your slides and let me say I am impressed with the findings."

"Okay," I returned without anything else to say.

"When Andrus asked for help, I was more than willing to try. I have been a pathologist for more than a lifetime and I have never seen anything like your blood. Like tar, I thought. It took us forever to get a good stain for our slide. Not your fault I'm sure, but damn tricky."

He didn't make sense to me. Try what? I think he was amused at the suggestion of helping out something so strange; no doubt that if there was a publishable case, he would be top on the medical journal. I must have been a very expensive joke.

"Elle is waiting for us, I believe, and we'll see what we can do."

He led us out of the office and back down the hall to another door on the left. Inside was a large laboratory with black countertops, fancy equipment, and microscopes. To the right sat a chair and a huge machine, wired with flowing tubes placed here to there, this way and that.

"Hey there," the cute girl from the front greeted us again. "I'm Elle Vann."

"Eleven?" I said questioning. The girl ignored it, but I could tell I hit an irritation of hers.

"Elle is our lead technologist on the graveyard shift." Lennox leaned over to my ear. "I like to keep the good ones."

I shivered a little.

"Not ready yet. There is some prep I need to do first." Elle talked me through the monitors and the graphs. I looked down at the scratch graph measuring my vitals. It continually scratched a few small hills, but no defined down/up line that I would see with a heartbeat.

Elle was cute, like 'adorable' cute. I would think her best friend was Hello Kitty. She was small, pocket size cute. Her short, black hair had a fun, blue strip down the side, and was cut all over the place, but Asian girls could get away with that when Americans just look like they try too hard.

"Shall we see what happens here?"

I panicked. "But the blood. Do you think I'll have another allergic reaction?"

Elle shrugged. "We washed the blood of any anti-coagulant—"

"You washed it?" I asked.

"Of course," she continued like this was completely normal, "so it should be clean of anything which you might react to. We've got O Neg, since we couldn't figure out a blood type with your ugly samples. What we're trying to do is extract what you have in your veins right now and replace it with this blood."

"And then what?"

"We all stare at you." Elle's eyes grew big, looking at me with those fun glasses before she broke into a smile.

"Whatever works." I exhaled as I crawled into the chair. Elle placed electrodes around to monitor other things, got out a mess of tubing and needles, and started cleaning my arms. Her phlebotomy skills were excellent and found a vein rather quickly, I'm guessing. The pain of the needle was more of a dull numbing ache. I watched as she did more prep work.

Andrus and Lennox stood chatting from a medical distance. With all my experience in doctors' offices, I couldn't figure out what they really talked about, but it was interesting.

"...the antibody is still reacting. I placed a drop of blood in the dish and the virus went wild. V is still prevalent in the system, but the hypercoagulation simply makes it impossible for the virus to do its job properly."

Elle turned on the machine and I lost the conversation. The tubes went around and round in a calming hum. The pull on my arm was not comfortable. The globs of blood in my veins were not ready to leave, so Elle tried regular saline to loosen up things. I couldn't think of anything more disgusting than seeing my veins trickle out black diluted clumps. The saline had worked some, so Elle tried to direct the blood in the other vein.

Then the pain came, and it was excruciating. My body didn't know what to do. All the sudden, nearly two weeks without blood in its system, here it was forcing its way in.

"Excuse me," Elle said from the machine. She walked over to my chest and slammed her fists down.

"Hey! What are you—"

"So sorry," she apologized again.

"Wait—" I tried to say, but she slammed me again.

"Without a beat it's hard to get everything around," she stated with another grunt.

"Here, let me," Nadia came up and took over the chest compressions, beating me harder, squeezing my chest.

I could feel the blood stop and pull around in my body, like sucking a thick shake through a straw, forcing its way where it shouldn't be. The burning sensation intensified in my limbs as it traveled downward. I clenched my teeth as the sensation increased around my body.

The machine tried to pump out my blood but kept jamming with clots. Elle would clamp and flush the line to help, but it slowed down the procedure.

Nadia watched the pain I was going through. I saw it in her sympathetic side glances as she continued slamming my chest.

The blood traveled close to my heart; I could feel the burn coming closer. I panicked and clenched my chest like I was going to have a heart attack. Elle called off Nadia as they both watched my reaction. The blood warmed and filled my heart chamber; it felt so strange to me, like experiencing love for the very first time. My head began to clear, and my body relaxed.

"Look at that," Nadia mentioned. "I see color in your cheeks."

"No kidding?" I was nervous still at what my body was doing, but finally let it do what it was doing.

Lennox smiled said something wicked. "I believe you have tasted your first blood, my boy."

I gulped. Whatever was happening to me felt really good. I hated to admit that I liked it.

"Would you like a cocktail?" Lennox offered something more to Andrus than to me. He walked over to a machine with a rounded door that opened from the bottom. Inside were small shelves rocking back and forth. He grabbed a flat bag full of yellow liquid and Andrus grinned.

"I'm always so glad to come up here," Andrus remarked. "You always have the good stuff."

"AB too. Fresh. Collected it two days ago." Lennox spiked it in one of its ports and drained the liquid into glasses. "I don't think this will harm you."

I took the glass with my unhooked arm and looked at it more intensely. "What is it?" The liquid swirled around in streaming ribbons of gold, like a painting of ornamental clouds.

"Platelets," Lennox smirked. "The sweetness of the blood. Vampires are so blinded by lust for blood they forget about the finer things."

I raised the glass to my lips, and the platelets trickled down my throat. It felt like spun honey in my mouth, and I smiled. A sense of my life was returning to me, and I felt happy.

Instead of relishing in on the platelet cocktail, Elle moved around the equipment. "Doctor, will you look at his vitals," she pointed out.

I had no clue about what she was talking about. I shouldn't have any vitals, but sure as anything I could feel it. I swear this time, it wasn't my imagination. I wasn't wishing it were true. As slight as a flap of a butterfly's wing, I could feel my heart trying to beat. I swore it. Was it the platelets or the clean blood filling my veins?

Lennox examined the paper scrolling off a small monitor. "The arrhythmia doesn't appear on the heart line. We have to consider the vibrations, and I imagine these indentations are from the clotted vein pulls, not from any Frankenstein experiment."

It didn't matter at this point. I knew what it was. She looked at me with a concerned face and shook her head slightly. I think she was sending me an unspoken message; this was something she didn't want to discuss with Lennox around. But the hairbrained idea of an antidote for this was too much to understand. I sank my head in the reality of it. Best to keep it a secret if I could.

She scribbled something on a piece of paper and discretely placed it in my pants pocket.

I didn't dare look at it until I came home.

The message had her phone number and read *I heard it too*.

9

HEALTHY APPEAL

"A MULTITUDE OF BOOKS DISTRACTS THE MIND."

I felt this strange new sensation surrounding me. It felt like hope, and it made me feel great. I had no idea what new blood was actually doing in my body. It wasn't circulating like normal blood, but I felt like it wanted to. Probably. It was enough of a difference that my depression started to lift. My outlook changed. For the first time I thought being a vampire might not be so bad. I might be okay with it.

I found Mitch zonked out on my couch when I returned, the controller still in his hand. I didn't want to rest, so I left and walked the streets by myself.

I eventually ended up back at the park where it all began, but at night it looked so different. It was only 3 a.m. and I felt great. I wanted to go for a run. I didn't care anymore what might happen to me. Me, a New York Vampire, I felt I could do anything.

I started to run. The clarity came when it was just me, my legs, and my music. I felt no physical change in my running ability. I wasn't super speedy or graceful, but me, running. I wasn't huffing and puffing like I would die, but my muscles cramped differently than before, not a hard burn, but a stiffness I couldn't shake out.

My thinking led me back to perhaps getting rid of it and returning to a normal life. The idea sounded impossible, however, nothing sounded impossible anymore. If vampires existed, then the possibility of becoming un-vampired could also exist, a logical and all-consuming conclusion.

I sat on the grass and watched the night sky fade in the morning light before I feared being outside with the sunshine and ran home.

It was three p.m. when I strolled into work. Beth immediately noticed the difference; I could see it in her face.

Deborah had Thursdays off, which meant I could use her computer; it ran so much faster than mine. I looked over my workload for the day. I still had a lot to do, but it just felt good to feel good again.

Beth, though I think she was trying to avoid me, kept looking up from her read and glancing in my direction.

"Here," Warren placed an interoffice mailer in front of me. "I got the microfilm from Dr. Weinsburgen. It needs to be scanned into…" he trailed off. I looked up at him and he was smiling. "You look better today, Brixby."

"Huh?"

"I mean; your color has returned."

"Oh, thanks," I sunk my head back down and looked over the envelope.

"If you want you can leave here at nine, if you're not inclined to stay late tonight."

"Sorry, I need the money," I responded with my head still down. He walked away and I lifted my head to see Beth staring at me. I caught her and she blushed.

"What?" I responded confused.

"Well," she started. "I'm just glad to see you looking better. Did you go running this morning?"

"You could say that," I answered.

"Well, I think it did you good. And I hope you started taking your meds again."

I didn't want to lie to her, but I was grateful for her concern, so I just smiled back.

"… and have you gone shopping lately?"

"Oh," I looked embarrassed. "I have a friend who picked it out."

"Is it a girl?"

I looked at her with a weird expression. Why was she bringing this up? "Maybe…"

"Figures," she huffed. "I didn't know you had a girlfriend. You never mentioned her before."

"I don't," I responded rather quickly.

She looked at me again. "Really?" A small smile crept to the corner of her mouth. "Okay. Then we should really have coffee sometime."

"Yeah, okay," I agreed. "But wait, aren't you dating someone?"

"This is just coffee," she entered. "Robert will be fine with this."

I have only ever liked Beth as a friend. There had never been an attraction there. I assumed it was mutual. Why now? There was no need for her to act so weird with me.

I ignored it and went back to work. After a few hours of scrolling through microfilm on the computer, my eyes started to strain. It felt good to take a break and stretch. I thought I might check out some new books to fill my mind from other ideas. I always loved sci-fi, but with the reality of my current situation, I didn't feel like reading it. Classic philosophy and theory might be too much thinking. I looked at the newest Dan Brown and it made my stomach sink—no religious thrillers either, just in case I'm damned.

I decided instead to skip finding a book and head downstairs to the faculty resource room to gather up more film.

On the first floor sat the juvenile section. Honestly, I had never browsed through it. I passed all the Harry Potters without a blink and shuffled past whatever whiny teen read was displayed. I often questioned why a sophisticated university like Hunter had a juvenile section anyway. It really never appealed to me.

But as I glanced briefly at the different books one book caught my eye.

Vampirologist:

A Study of the Fallen Ones

I stopped and smiled a little. The artwork on the front was very compelling, made to look like an old, ancient bible with a wicked vampire sucking the life out of some innocent damsel. A rye smile cornered my mouth as I opened it and fingered through the different pictures. My curiosity of how true is "the True History" fed my interest.

"Like Vampires?" a voice said to me.

I jumped a little, feeling embarrassed.

A person standing by a shelf of paranormal fiction smiled rather cute at me. The girl had to be a freshman, too young to attend grown-up college, but looked intelligent with her smart glasses and no-fuss brown hair pulled back into a ponytail. Why would she be down here looking over this teenage garbage?

"Just wondering how 'True' it is," I replied honestly.

"I think it's rather subjective really," she started. "It should be up to the reader. True or un-true, you know. Someone's fantasy could be alive, living in the realm of its creator. Don't you think?"

"Real to the person who believes it, but not actual fact. Brilliant." I wanted to debate her ridiculous point, but I was kind of charmed.

"But all stories have a basic nucleus. Even tabloid stories have a strand of truth."

I smiled. "With all things considered, you are telling me you believe this."

Her eyes intensified with a strange appeal. "I'm saying that there is no harm in believing in it, if you'd like."

This cynical side of my personality came out, thinking of gullible people filling hopes with fairy tales. But here came my reality check—I knew the truth about vampires and my ideals flipped into possibilities.

"How much do you know about vampires?" I asked, some out of curiosity, the other part stemmed from general appeal.

She smirked. "Enough." I think she was too embarrassed to tell me.

"Tell me this, then. Are you the Anne Rice type or the Stephenie Meyer type?"

She remained silent.

Gertrude from the Biological Science Library across the way looked at us with concern. I guess we talked too loud for a library.

The girl went back to the shelves, and I finished flipping through the book and put it back. As I headed for the stairs, a hand caught me.

"If you're looking for something interesting to read, I suggest this."

I looked over and the girl held out a book. By the cover I could tell this was definitely something I would never read.

"Uh… thanks." I took the book with me and headed back up the stairs.

When I got back to my desk, I examined the book more carefully. The cover had the bare back of a woman with marking tattoos down her spine. The back cover read something about forbidden love and a chance of redemption and renewal. Yuck, a romance. Like I would expect this girl to really pick out something I would enjoy.

I looked over at Beth a few desks down who was packing up her things, ready to head home.

"Beth, have you read this?" I held up the book.

"Coven Sisters? Very popular choice," she said mocking. "Didn't think you were the romantic-paranormal type."

"Me either," I returned.

I opened it and brushed through the pages. That's when a little pink slip of paper fell out. It was one of the slips for checking out archived material. On the back there was written a name with a message:

Sunnie Knight

744-555-3834

Everything this afternoon felt so strange. I'd become suddenly attractive, that job had always been reserved for Mitch, but here were three—if you count Warren—signals of interest in me. Maybe being a vampire had its benefits.

My curious came out and I went to peek where the girl was, if she was still here. I caught her heading across the walk toward the bridge. I quickly pulled out my sunglasses just to check.

Nope. She was definitely human.

10

DATING—THE VAMPIRE WAY

"BEAUTY IS A SHORT-LIVED TYRANNY."

"This is dangerous territory, Parker," Nadia said to me on the other end of the phone. I rang her once I left work. "You don't want to be dating humans. It doesn't turn out well. Trust me on this one, Park, this is beyond stupid."

She was right, but I didn't like hearing it. I had my own personal reasons: if I, in fact, could reverse my vampirism, this wouldn't be a problem. Nadia had been really good to me, my best friend through these past weeks, but I didn't like the tone she used when I asked her such a simple question.

"And I just asked if there were any vampire-friendly restaurants around," I returned. "I didn't ask for dating advice." I worried that I offended her, and Nadia was the last person I'd want as an enemy. "Sorry, I don't know anything different, you know? I'm trying to work things out, that's all."

"Call Jovanny, he'd know," she suggested. "And if you want dating advice, talk to him. He's full of advice." She hung up on me. Not a good sign. I didn't think I had been that rude.

Jovanny was glad I called but still worried about my condition. The place he suggested was called Nosferatu, in Greenwich Village. It was a hot spot for New York Vampires out for fun, but he cautioned it sometimes can get ugly for humans.

"Its vibe is on the creepy side," Jovanny stated on the phone. "There are some pretty gothic artifacts on the walls, and people tend to get nervous in the atmosphere. And it can be a little trendy with the quote-un-quote gothic crowd, but the drinks are killer."

"If you found a date, would you want to join me?"

"Hell yes!"

And it was set. Jovanny and Mitch both agreed to come. It had been a long time since I had truly gone out with a girl. I wasn't social. I used the excuse of collegiate aptitude, but with that pretty much finished and my new un-life ahead of me, anything seemed possible. Now I just had to build up my nerve to call this girl Sunnie.

Friday was busy. I had only two weeks until finals, and I felt a little panicked for my Anthropology class, and I shouldn't really care, but that part of my personality would never die I'm afraid. I ran around a little in the afternoon and stopped by the Wexler, even though I didn't work, just in hopes she might be there. But she wasn't. Time was slipping and I needed to call her.

"Hello," it was a sweet voice, like she had been working in customer service for years.

"Am I speaking with Sunnie?"

"Uh, huh," she answered. "Can I ask who's calling?"

"I got your message."

It went quiet. "Who is this?"

"On a pink slip of paper, in a book that, sorry to tell you, I doubt I'll read."

I heard the smile behind the voice. "Sorry," she tried to collect herself. "I can't believe you called me."

"Why?"

"Because, I have never done anything so stupid in my life, I mean..." she trailed off. "I mean, I'm really glad that you did, but I thought for sure I was out of your league."

"Really?" This struck me as funny. I could say the same about her.

"Sorry, now I just feel like an idiot."

"Stop making yourself feel bad and come to dinner with me." It went silent. I might have dropped the call. "Hello?"

"Yes... sorry... yes..." she repeated.

"I'm Oliver, by the way."

"Can't wait to meet you, Oliver."

The phone call was brief, but enough. I got her information and planned to meet her around eight.

Mitch had Tivoli around his arm, and Jovanny asked Nadia to come. Even though she hung up on me, I felt better having her there. I didn't think she was mad, but it was possible.

I decided to walk down to Sunnie's apartment and meet the others at the restaurant. She lived near campus, and it was a nice night for a walk. I really had no other plans in my head. I hadn't thought about what I would be eating or how I was going to act. I just hoped to be charming and myself and see how things went.

When I knocked on the door of her twelfth-floor apartment, my stomach sank. This was crazy. Not only did I not know this girl, but I was inviting her to party with vampires. I must be out of my mind. I almost turned when the door opened.

This girl was not the same girl, or if it was, I had completely misjudged her. Her hair was down and smooth, swept over out of her face. She still had her cute, brown-rimmed glasses, but she looked so much older than I originally thought. Even with my new clothes, I still felt like a slob next to her clean, pressed black button-down dress.

"Oliver?" she held out her hand in greeting.

"Yes, and you are Sunnie?"

"Serafina Knight, my real name, but my dad called me Sunnie, because I brightened his day." My thinking at this moment—*I might vomit.* "That's why I rebelled and fell in love with vampires."

Phew. "Sunnie Knight is rather a contradiction," I replied.

"It gives the wrong impression of me."

"Should I be worried?"

She just gave a coy smile as she turned to lock her door, but by her demeanor, she wasn't a contradiction. her personality was as bright as her name.

We grabbed a taxi on the way down to the restaurant and talked.

I learned Sunnie was from Upper Peninsula Michigan, a history major in her second year at Hunter, and a hater of girlie things.

"I feel uncomfortable around others wearing pink," she laughed. "Even pastels can sometime be offensive. Floral is totally out."

I snickered at her adamant passion against femininity. "Do you hate soft, fluffy things too, like bunnies?"

"What? No…" she trailed off. "Though, I don't have much experience with them."

I think she missed my joke." So, you must be a skull-loving Hello Kitty wearer."

"Maybe," her word turned up at the end. "She looks great in plaid." I think I might have embarrassed her. "Tell me about you, Oliver. Where are you from?"

"Jersey," I hated that answer. "Nothing special about me. I don't have a very interesting history."

"New Jersey isn't that bad. I mean, it's not far. I've been there a few times."

"A few times doesn't give you that lingering taste in your mouth."

"Well, you're a book lover."

"Uh, yes, but not of whatever book you handed me."

She laughed with a smile. "It was just what was in front of me."

"So, you haven't read it?"

"No, I've read it, but it wasn't one of my favorites. A bit contrived. Do you like gothic fiction?"

"Oh no," I said without thinking. "I'll stick with post-Socratic reads." She looked lost. "Paranormal fiction is cool. I think it's fascinating that someone can think of all that, but I am interested in folklore behind it and what have you. There seems like there are so many interpretations of the genre." As I was speaking it, it all started losing meaning. I felt like a hypocrite.

"Not many guys do," she answered. "I was glad to see you down in the Juvi books. I figured you were too intellectual for that section."

"I pretend," I kidded. "Do you go to the Wexler often?"

"Yes. I've seen you there, hiding on the second floor."

"Really?"

"Of course. For my History of Economics class, I had to look up old articles on the 1930 Economic Summit Reconstruction, and you helped me."

"Oh, I don't remember. If it was in the fall, I helped a lot of kids." Now *I* was the one embarrassed.

"But it wasn't until I saw you looking at that 'Vampirologist' book that I thought you would ever go out with me."

Her talk charmed me, and I hated to admit that I was a little touched by the effort. "I may go check out that book," I admitted.

We both laughed. But the truth was, I was most definitely going back and checking out that book.

The rest of the ride we playfully chatted about nothing. It felt like a normal activity, to be happy.

But when I reached the restaurant, my stomach hit the bottom. What was I doing? What was I thinking? I should have checked out this place before I brought her. What if something happened to her? Out of all the people who might like to become a vampire, I picked right.

A small overhanging sign read Nosferatu in gold scrolling letters. It didn't look much different from other places I've visited in the city. The place was crowded outside. A line of people waited, talking and mingling pleasantly.

Mitch was outside with Tivoli, and I made a quick introduction.

"Mitch has been my best friend for, I don't know how long."

"Sixth grade," Mitch mentioned. "I beat him up, but then my mom made me apologize, and when I went over to his house, I found out he had a Nintendo 64, and we became friends."

"Thanks for the awful flashback of my childhood," I said to him dryly.

Sunnie didn't mind. She turned to me. "You know; I've always wanted to go here."

"I thought, due to our introduction, you might enjoy a place like this."

"Do you know who Nosferatu was?"

"Not really," I answered honestly.

"Back in the nineteen twenties, there was a movie called 'Nosferatu—Eine Symphonies das Grauens—'" the German rolled off her tongue. "Or Symphony of Horror. It's a movie that blatantly rips off Bram Stoker's Dracula, storyline, characters, and everything. In 1979, they remade it, but it was still pretty awful. The earliest Hollywood depiction of vampires comes from that early movie. You know, the creepy guy with the long fingers and bug-eyes. That's him."

"Wow, I am impressed," I started. "This was my friend's idea. I've never been here."

Sunnie smiled. "I just hope the food is better than the movie."

Jovanny and Nadia came out of the door hailing us. Nadia still had a concerned look on her face.

"There is a table for us," she said and walked back inside.

"Is she mad at you?" Sunnie picked up.

"Yeah, seems that way," I replied.

As we walked inside, the place changed to a dark, smoky atmosphere. Thick, black fabric lined the walls, candelabras lit the narrow hallway past small tables placed here and there. Light, muffled chats lifted around us and absorbed in the fabric.

"Here you are," the hostess guided us to a round table with large candles and intricate plates and dinnerware. I immediately felt the dent in my wallet. I didn't know if I could afford being a vampire.

We got menus, and I couldn't believe it. There were salads and other regular menu items with chicken and smothered stuff. Then there was a menu entitled: Blutrünstig—the specialty menu. The listed dishes and drinks all had very bloody tastes—Blood pudding, blood sausage, on and on.

"Is this where you got your ideas?" I asked Nadia impressed, looking over the interesting menu items listed.

She smiled and went back down to her menu. I think she might forgive me… maybe…

I looked over at Sunnie. I had forgotten that she had no idea about us vampires. I second guessed my comment to Nadia, and I needed to be more careful. Sunnie looked unaware and continued to glance over the menu.

Our waiter appeared. He looked no different than any other waiter you might find at a nice restaurant. I was disappointed. I imagined he would be dressed more theatrically for such a place.

"What are you interested in?" I leaned over to Sunnie.

"I don't care much for meat," she whispered to me. "I think I'm just going to get a salad this time, until I see what these dishes are."

"I agree," I returned. How I wished I could have met her earlier, both us vegetarians. Those ideals kept slipping through my mind. The blood thing hadn't solidified in my brain yet.

As I looked over the items, I grew nervous. What if I have some kind of reaction again? I looked at Nadia with pleading in my eyes.

As she ordered, she added, "…and Parker here will have the Xidato Filets, very rare with a clean V-8."

I smiled in gratitude, but Sunnie was glaring at me. "Parker?"

"Oh, sorry, that's just a nickname Nadia has for me. I remind her of Peter Parker."

"Spiderman?" she asked and turned to Nadia. "You've got to tell me why."

Nadia smirked in a wicked way. "Peter Parker seems like a regular guy, but he hides a big secret."

"Oh." Sunnie leaned to me. "You must tell me."

"Not on the first date," I kidded. I felt a kick from under the table and looked across to Nadia, who smiled to herself as she grew more interested in the wine list.

The subject dropped for the moment.

Little conversations popped up about random stuff. Mitch was telling some unbelievable story to impress Tivoli, who seemed intrigued, and Jovanny kept interjecting with his also incredible tales, all topping Mitch's. Sunnie seemed to enjoy herself. She liked hearing these stories, especially if they involved me.

As the talk went on, I went into my observation mode, which happened all the time, and I began studying the way Jovanny and Nadia interacted.

It was very clear Jovanny liked her, the way he reacted, always trying to include her in his stories. He was very expressive and seemed to touch her arm excessively. I wasn't bothered, or was I? As I said before, she can date whoever she liked, but Jovanny seemed unlikely to be her type. He was eccentric and weird, with his love for comic books and action figures; Nadia was pristine and sharp, clever and beautiful. He seemed so far out of her league. I also noticed her general irritation with things that he said.

And it shouldn't bother me—it shouldn't. I don't know why it did. Here I was with a great girl, but she was human. Nadia was a great girl also, but the more I got to know her, I think I would be in the same line as Jovanny if I tried for her. I needed to stay in my comfort zone—and Sunnie fit perfectly in that zone.

The food arrived wheeled on a cart. The server handed it out one by one. If you were observing the feast, who could tell who was a vampire and who was not. I could see the bloody soup mess on Jovanny's plate; the large sausage mass oozing with blood gravy in front of Tivoli; the large steak, mildly rare before Mitch, and Sunnie's ginger salad. My own plate was a bloody mess—it looked like a Greek gyro with bloody pig's feet. I guess with the success of bacon it wouldn't be so bad.

I looked at Nadia's plate and almost laughed. A large pomegranate lay sliced open with creamy sauces drizzled around swimming seeds.

"Going for dessert first?" I said candidly.

"I know what I want, Park, and I don't like to waste my time."

"Tell me what this is?"

Nadia smiled. "It's a fried Pomegranate, caramelized and set with um… I'm not quite sure." she trailed off looking over at Sunnie next to me, who was picking at her salad. She lowered her voice. "I'll let you taste it later."

My first bite was good. I sucked the blood through my teeth very slowly. I didn't like chewing. It had been a while since I tried to eat, and I felt that my tongue had forgotten how. My teeth weren't sharp like fangs, so I didn't have any difficulty there. But slowly, the blood came from the meat as I chewed, and my satisfaction increased.

My drink was not V-8. Clean V-8 is a code for the cleanest, purest, freshest blood. I don't know where it came from and didn't care. It tasted wonderful.

Sunnie asked about our different dishes. She seemed most intrigued by Nadia's like us all. "I didn't see that on the menu at all."

"I know the chef," she answered. She again made eyes at me, but this time they were softer.

Sunnie noticed this time, and as a response placed her hand on my knee. I hid my surprise and tried again to focus on my food.

I got another kick in the shin.

When dinner ended and the bill was paid, Sunnie turned to me. "So, are we going dancing?"

"Umm… sure." I answered without processing her request. I wasn't a dancer.

"Do you guys want to go?" she asked the others. Mitch and Tivoli were up for it, but Nadia bailed, taking Jovanny with her.

This was good though. I was here with a normal girl having a normal time. For the brief moment, I felt normal. I felt better than normal. I felt better than me. This wasn't me; this was the new me, much better than that whining, sad, allergy ridden nobody.

Tonight, I felt like a New York Vampire.

Right before I puked in the alley outside the dance club.

11

THE TRUTH ABOUT SULFA

"WHERE THERE IS REVERENCE THERE IS FEAR, BUT THERE IS NOT REVERENCE EVERYWHERE THAT THERE IS FEAR, BECAUSE FEAR PRESUMABLY HAS A WIDER EXTENSION THAN REVERENCE."

Elle was contacted immediately. I didn't want to tell Nadia, and I wasn't sure why. I felt like she might be disappointed in me, like she was right or something. Which, to be fair, she might be, but I didn't want to tell her that.

Mitch took me home. He told Sunnie I must have had too much to drink. She didn't like not being invited to help. I really think she had fun with me, but she couldn't come. I needed to figure this out myself.

Elle Vann, from the Sleepy Hollow Blood Bank, was working the graveyard shift at the time I called. She promised to contact me when Lennox wasn't around. I wasn't really sure why, but I guessed involving Lennox was rather risky. She said she would help, and I was pleased not to deal with creepy

Lennox. Around three in the morning she rang. From what I told her she sounded concerned.

"Your body is rejecting something," she said from the other side of the phone. "Vampires don't get sick or throw up. I can't figure out what it could be without further investigation. What exactly did you eat?"

"Well, I'm not really sure," I answered sheepish. "Nadia was the one who ordered for me."

"We'll have to contact her."

"What about the restaurant?" I came in quickly.

"Yes, that is an option, but I think Nadia will know more."

She was right. Nadia knew more than anyone else, I guessed.

"Would you like me to phone her?" Elle asked.

It would be nice not to deal with her grouchiness toward me, but I needed to find out. "Thanks for offering, but I'll call. I think I need to apologize anyway."

Mitch and Tivoli left me alone to figure out my misery. I figured Tivoli was sick of helping me. She didn't care about the situation at all, just out there to have a good time and use my best friend. As I said before—Man-eater.

When I dialed Nadia, she didn't answer. I left a message but didn't have much hope. About five minutes later there was a buzz at my door.

I answered.

Nadia stood there all alone. I looked surprised, but she didn't.

"Sorry, Ollie, for coming over so late, can I come in?"

I couldn't believe it. "Please!" I nearly hugged her, but . . . didn't.

She went to the window and looked down at the street.

"I just called you."

"Yes, I saw that."

"Did you listen to the message?"

"Yes. I was outside your door. I've been there for a half an hour."

This was strange. I wanted to help her, find out whatever bothered her. This wasn't the same girl that made me a Bacon Smoothie. This girl had lost her sparkle somewhere.

"Nadia, are you okay?" I was concerned, but also confused. "And why did you call me 'Ollie?'" I said for no reason. She had called me Parker for the last few weeks. It must be serious.

A slight smile crossed her lips. "Oliver, I came here to—" she got stuck on her words. "I came here to apologize."

"Huh?" This was big. "It was just a date. I know that you didn't like the idea of me going out with a human but—"

"It's not that—" she cut me off. "Well, not really that. She seems very sweet, really. It is true that I didn't like, well don't like the idea, but that is not—" She turned around and sat on the couch. I followed out of concern.

"If it's not Sunnie, then I'm very confused," I started. "I think you have been more than helpful since... you know. And I can't figure why you would need to apol—"

"Stop. Please," Nadia came back. "Don't be so nice to me." She took a deep breath before continuing. "I feel I've done something really awful to you and I'm sorry."

"Okay?"

"I spiked your drink tonight."

"With what?"

"Bactrim."

I felt nauseous just sitting there. When she said the words, I didn't know what to say. I was in shock. It felt like a knife twisting at my deepest wounds in my worst memories. "Why would you do that?"

"I had a good reason."

I sputtered in confusion. "It was just a date! Nothing else. It's not like I plan on marrying the girl. I just wanted to go out—"

"Stop! Ollie! Let me finish—"

"Did you want me to look stupid? Because I did. I really did. Puking out everything right in front of the club, where everyone could see me. It was a huge, bloody mess, like a crime scene, and does not clean up as easily as Dexter makes it look. We had to just leave it. Were you trying to sabotage me? Did—" she covered my mouth with her hand.

"Ollie, I like you, so shut up."

I grumbled the rest of my words under her fingers, but then sat silently waiting for the explanation.

"After the red cell exchange, I talked with Elle, and we thought we might experiment."

I pried her fingers from my mouth. "You talked to her earlier?" That sneak!

"I have been communicating with her ever since your transfusion. We are trying to keep Andrus and Lennox both out of this. If Lennox found out what we were doing, he would be upset."

"Why?"

Nadia leaned her back against the pillows on my couch." He doesn't want to give you the chance to become human again."

"Is that what you are doing?"

"Well, I think we figured it out." She pulled out some papers from her bag. Notes and scribbles littered the pages, and a few with medical slide pictures with purplish blobs.

"Sorry, I'm missing it," I stated stupidly.

"TMP Sulfa."

"What about it?"

"It's possible Sulfa is protecting you, preventing you from becoming, like me."

"I don't get it."

"Ollie, you *were* having a reaction that morning when you were attacked. Something in your blood protected you, preventing the change. Look," she pulled over some of the papers. "Here is a picture of a normal blood smear. I added some of my own saliva enzymes to the sample and watched the reaction. The enzymes are attracted to the platelets in the blood first on the way to the marrow. I'm not sure why. Platelets are naturally sweeter. I know. I've had them. So, I researched." She pulled out more papers. "You can become thrombocytopenic when having a reaction to sulfa drugs. Which means your platelet level goes down? I did a smear of your blood that first day and look," she pulled out another purplish blob. "These white dots. You hardly had any platelets to react from."

I was speechless, and very confused.

"But that really is only part of the problem. The reason why your body acted the way it did is still a mystery. Science can only take us so far here."

"So, what does this mean? That I'm not a real vampire? I'm half and half?"

"I don't know," she said quietly.

My mind wrapped around the thought. I felt like she just told me I had cancer. "I can't be like this," I finally said, exasperated of any thought. "I can't be half. That doesn't mean anything. Everything I've ever heard or read about vampires is total crap. Holy water, reflections, silver bullets—"

"I think that's werewolves—"

"You know what I mean," I corrected. "This is not the glamorous vampire lifestyle."

"But the blood exchange worked."

"Basically, you are telling me I need to be on dialysis. That whatever I do, I'll always have to continually be on a machine the rest of my existence?"

Nadia sat back again, her head resting on her anchored arm. "I have a theory."

I humored her for a moment.

"It has to do with the exchange. Elle said you felt something."

I brought my head back up. "What do you mean?" I asked.

"I was curious of the arrhythmia and asked Elle about it. It is an anomaly for sure, but we have never had to deal with this. We think your state is not permanent."

"And I can be human again?"

"Or a zombie. We don't know."

That impossibility came back: a normal life again.

"But can I ask you a question?" Nadia asked.

"Okay?"

"Even if you were to go back to being human, would you want to?"

"Of course," I answered. It was an automatic response to tell the truth.

"But your life as a human was miserable, all the health problems and medications. If we could remove the sulfa and make you a vampire, would you do that?"

"Nadia, that doesn't make sense. Why would I want to be anything but human?"

She looked at me with a forlorn expression. What was she getting at? "We'll try some experiments." She smiled again and placed her hand on my knee, "and sorry for sabotaging your date."

I nodded and smiled back. "She wasn't ready for that place."

Nadia laughed. "With all the vampire novels she's read, I thought she would have a stronger stomach. I honestly thought she was going to pass out when they brought you your food."

And there was the Nadia I admired. It felt good to have her on my side again. "Don't worry about it. She'll have to come around to the idea eventually, right?"

"Unless it works," Nadia answered. "You are still going to go out with her?"

"Sure," I answered. "She's sweet."

She smirked but didn't say much about it. "Next Wednesday, Parker," she said as she stood up to leave. "Another blood exchange."

"Got it," I returned.

As I opened the door, Nadia did something unexpected— she hugged me.

"I'm glad you're all right," she whispered. "I didn't like giving you that drink."

"Understand," I resigned, and she left.

12

LARPS

"I WAS AFRAID THAT BY OBSERVING OBJECTS
WITH MY EYES AND TRYING TO COMPREHEND
THEM WITH EACH OF MY OTHER SENSES I
MIGHT BLIND MY SOUL ALTOGETHER."

After Nadia left, I decided to go on a walk. The weather felt good and the sun came so early in New York, I had better get out before it.

My body felt weary. The vomiting episode took a little out of me, like stomach flu, but the air on my face felt refreshing. The street noise of New York helped drown out any convoluted banter happening inside my head. My mind wandered backward, processing everything Nadia had told me. The possibility was amazing. What if I could return to normal and forget this whole mess ever happened?

In my walk, I peered over to the grove of trees where the girl first attacked me. I avoided it last time, too emotionally drawn. But this time I ran directly for it. I didn't like avoiding it. It was a lovely spot in the park. But I slowed down when I reached the path and looked around. It was so peaceful, other than a few nightingales chirping. I admired the rock where the girl jumped at me. My feet covered the path exactly where the first bite came, the bite that ended my life.

I felt hurt again, replaying that dreadful morning. I shouldn't care anymore, even if I could somehow be changed back. I remembered once feeling pity for her.

I moved toward the meadow and stopped to lie down on the grass and smelled. That's right, I smelled the grass. You know what? I loved the smell of grass. Grass and I were enemies. I hated grass. I wasn't allowed to play soccer as a child with my allergies and asthma. I couldn't recall a time when I just lay down like this without blankets, long sleeves, long pants, Claritin.

I sat up and began pulling at the grass like a child. It did feel good to rub my fingers in the cool strands.

I looked up, back toward the grove of trees. I might have seen movement, but my eyes could easily be playing tricks on me in the weird night light. Searching again I did see something. It wasn't my peripheral vision tricking me, I saw something—a figure.

I quickly got up. A flash of dark curls caught my attention. I squinted for a better look. There was definitely someone there, and I felt their eyes staring back at me.

I had her.

I began running towards her as fast as I could back to the grove.

The figure also began to run, dodging this way and that through the trees, but I was there on her heels. I could see where she was going.

The grove opened. The figure darted under a tunnel bridge. She was trapped. I had her.

As the arch grew closer, I slowed down. I felt invincible as a vampire should. Who could kill me? Who could harm me?

She had to be around here. My eyes searched the tunnel. The scurrying of little critters echoed lightly along the ground. She had to be here. I approached the brick wall but couldn't find anything. The other side of the tunnel was empty. How could I have lost her? She was just here.

A crunch on sticks came from behind me. I whipped around to an empty park. I felt the presence of someone nearby. Maybe I had Spidey-sense. Maybe I was Peter Parker. I turned in a circle surveying all around. She had to be here.

Suddenly someone dropped behind me. An arm tightened around my throat, accompanied by a sharp blade aimed directly at my chest.

"You are a trespasser here," a gruff voice said in my ear. From my peripheral vision I spotted two more shapes coming toward me. They were covered head to foot with draped cloaks, each brandishing a long sword, serious swords, in their hands.

"Leave here or die," the voice started to crack, a slight laugh stifled in his throat.

"Are you kidding me?" escaped my mouth.

"We don't like your kind here," again he began to laugh. Then the others lowered their swords and began to laugh.

The arm loosened, and I quickly turned to face my attacker.

He also was wearing a long cloak with the hood pulled up, but he lowered it and I saw the cool, long hair that belonged to Jovanny.

"What are you doing out here?" I said to him. "You scared me to death."

"If that was possible," he returned. "This is Algar and Barnold of the Eastern River."

"Hi, I'm Seth," the first one reached out in greeting.

"Tim," the other one waved.

"Algar and Barnard?" I clarified, not understanding the two names.

"LARP characters. Come." He slapped me on the shoulder and led me forward back in the tunnel with very little explanation. In the tunnel, by the brick I had just examined, Jovanny simply moved his hand over a few bricks and pushed something—a door. It opened up to a little room lit with a few gas lanterns. A table sat positioned in the middle with a large map of the park. There were role-playing books around and different shaped dice.

"This is our Lair," Jovanny commented. "Come in."

I sat down on a very old, moldy-looking couch, still weirded out by where I was. "What are you guys doing here?"

"LARP, man," Seth, or Algar, as his LARP name would be, said. "Best sport in the world."

"What is that again?" I asked.

"Live Action Role Playing, RPG like Dungeons & Dragons, but real."

"Real, huh?" I returned unnerved.

"We tend to get our ideas in here and then take them to the Park," Tim, or Barnold, returned. "It's such a rush to get people involved. They think we're going to mug them or something. That will give those tourists something to talk about."

"Interesting," I said, but it gave me an idea. "Do you do this all the time?"

"About every weekend," Jovanny answered. "I promised to meet Tim around midnight, that's the best time when the town hasn't gone to bed yet. We can get some serious fighting in. Nadia knew I was coming here. I never miss my Friday LARP. Personally, I think she was in a bad mood."

I had the upper hand on this conversation and smiled to myself.

"Well, maybe you can help me then," I asked. "I'm looking for a girl. I swear I saw her come this way."

"A girl?" Seth sniggered. "What would she be doing in the park this late?"

"She's not just a girl, she's like—" I stopped myself. Were these guys vampires, or just eccentric weirdoes? "She's like, what, like Jovanny is, I guess."

"Good looking and awesome," Jovanny punched Seth in the arm as they laughed.

"No, I mean she's a—"

"Vampire?" Tim answered. "Cool."

"These guys are cool," Jovanny clarified. "They're vamps too."

"This girl is the one who attacked me and—"

"Whoa," Jovanny entered. "There better not be any retaliation. I don't do that."

"I'm curious, that's all," I tried to sound positive. "Small, teenage type, dark wild curls, and I swear I saw her over in the grove by the lake."

"Interesting," Jovanny contemplated my request. "Sounds like fun, something we three could handle. Is there money involved?"

"You want me to pay you?"

He thought about it, "Nah, not really, it's just my character's nature to be greedy with coin! Aha!" He made a very valiant stab with his sword in my direction and then sat back down. "Yeah, we can do it."

13

ON THE ROOFTOP

"ONCE MADE EQUAL TO MAN, WOMAN BECOMES HIS SUPERIOR."

Three in the afternoon my phone rang. It could have rung a couple times, but I was barely coherent enough to recognize it was the phone at all. Some obnoxious song came on as my ringtone, a prank from Mitch because I never lock my phone. I had to remember to change that.

"Hello," I answered, trying my best "No you didn't wake me—I've been awake for hours" voice.

"Oliver?"

If my heart could beat, it would have stopped. "Mom?" I didn't mean it to be a question. I should have expected her to call, but honestly, it was the last thing on my mind.

"Oliver. Thank goodness. I tried your number and it didn't work. But your father gave me your new number. When did you get a new number?"

"It's been about two years, Mom," I clarified. My mother, sweet housewife Shirley Ann Brixby, had a hard time remembering any changes in life. Tell her something once, she'll remember, but change anything after that, it would never stay in her memory for long. I remember having three different dogs in my life, all named Dexter, because even though I named the second Leroy and our third, Harvey, it didn't matter to her, they were all Dexter. I thought she just liked the name, but when I was a teen, I made the connection that she didn't know it was a different dog.

"Well, I'm just glad you're all right," she started. Her sweet, upturned voice instantly reminded me of Saturday morning filled with warm oatmeal and brown sugar. She began rambling about some slightly relatable story about how my Aunt Margaret's neighbor didn't answer her phone, just to find out she had been dead for three days. My mother often worried about those things happening to everyone.

I kept in the conversation saying "Yep" and "Uh-huh" a few times before I really caught what she was talking about. "Wait a second…You're coming?"

"Well, of course sweetie. Your father and I will be there to support you. I'm actually excited. I haven't been to New York City since—"

"Wait, when are you coming?"

"Well, you said it was around two when it started on the twelfth."

"I did?"

"It has been a few weeks since we talked, but I wouldn't think it had changed. Has it changed?"

"Uh. I… don't think so…" Honestly, what was she talking about?

"I'm glad. I can't wait to see you with your cap and everything."

The conversation started to spark ticks of memory in my brain—a conversation that happened only days before my attack.

Ah, crap! Graduation was the furthest thing from my mind. It had been my life. How could I become so absentminded to forget the whole ceremony and hoopla that goes with it?

"Mom. Mom," I tried to interrupt her. "I don't know if I'm going to my graduation. I think I've changed my mind. Who really needs to walk anyway?"

A fit of fury came from this sweet woman's mouth. I tried to calm her down, but I didn't know what to say. My graduation from college was a big deal for my mild-mannered parents. Their only child, their hope for the future, their "Big City Son" as my dad would call me, now had an uncertain future and a secret he would have to tell them.

Or would I? I looked at the calendar. The twelfth of May, a Friday, was nearly two weeks away. Was that enough time for my non-human/human experiment to happen?

"You know what, Mom, don't worry about it. Let's talk about the details of your coming later. Right now, I need to go."

"Oliver, this is a big deal to us. Your father won't travel that way unless it is important. So, I want to go to dinner, and I might want to see a play—"

"Mom," I interrupted. "Sorry, I understand. Big deal, I got it. I'll call you later, okay?"

"And were you going to come for Nana's eightieth birthday?"

It was impossible to hang up with this woman. "I'll see what I can do," I said. "Love you, Mom, bye-bye," and hung up.

This complicated everything.

Mitch came over directly after I talked with my mom and brought me a raw T-Bone to replace the one he ate. I cubed it and sucked each piece dry.

Around five my phone buzzed with a text message.

Meet me at the Wexler @ 7:45

I looked at the number but didn't recognize it. I wasn't working today, and I'd rather not show my face there if I could help it. "Do you know this number?" I asked Mitch.

"Nope," he said with his mouth stuffed with Cheetos. "Maybe it's your girlfriend."

"Or maybe it's Beth," I said with a creepy feeling in my stomach about her idea of coffee." I texted back

– And you are?

...Buzz... 7:45 sharp Parker

It was Nadia. No problem. She probably had more information for me or something. I had no plans and maybe she could help me figure out my Parent dilemma.

It was dusk when I left. Hunter campus was swimming with excitement. I had forgotten all the End of School celebrations that went on. I might have been there, even though I in nature am not a party person, I would have attempted to have fun for the sake of my finishing college. As I observed, I envied the simplicity of it all; the girls in less than casual clothes, flirting in inconspicuous ways—it would be fun to join. A few buddies from my Tech Writing class hailed me as I walked by. I waved and went on. The seriousness of my situation prevented me from even attempting fun.

The Wexler closed at eight, which didn't leave much time. I walked in and immediately went downstairs avoiding any contact with Deborah, the cat lady. Down in Juvi again. Nobody should come here on a Saturday night. I looked around at some of the covers of the books—honestly some looked cute. Then I glanced back at the Vampire books and glimpsed *Vampirologist*. I wanted to check this book out, so I opened it and glanced at some of the information it had.

"Honestly, what is your fascination with that book?"

I looked up. Sunnie stood right in front of me. "Where did you come from?" And I meant it. The place was empty, and she materialized out of nowhere. It took me by surprise.

"Must be a pretty gripping read if you didn't notice me," she stated. "I followed you in."

"What are you doing here?" I asked. I really didn't want her to be here when Nadia showed up. It would complicate matters, and I didn't like the explanation that might come. Wasn't it bad enough that I had to tell my parents?

"Meeting you," she smiled. "You got my text."

"That was you?"

"My phone died, and I borrowed my roommates."

"Clever," I retorted and closed the book. "How did you know where I would go?"

She smiled again. "Our little vampire conversation is not over."

"Oh, really," I stated, but honestly, a slight bit nervous.

The overhead came on telling us the library was about to close.

"Come on, let's go—" I tried to say, but she quickly put her hand over my mouth and smiled wickedly.

Without saying a word, she grabbed my hand and pulled me back to a corner. There was a secluded little alcove with a small desk.

"What are you—" I tried to say through her hand, but it sounded muffled.

"Shh…" she said. "It'll be fun."

"Are you trying to get me fired?"

"What do you care? You're graduating."

She was right, but it was against my ethical code.

The lights went slowly down one by one. I sensed a person coming down and looking around Juvi, but then the stair door shut. A few moments later we were alone.

"You're out of your mind, you know," I whispered once she lowered her hand.

"Meh," she shrugged. "I just like to be a little adventurous sometimes. Come on, loosen up Park—"

"Could you not call me Parker?" I interrupted.

"But Nadia can?"

"Nadia has her reasons that I don't really agree with," I said. It bothered me a little. I felt tricked, thinking I was meeting Nadia. "She's making fun of me, and I'd rather you didn't."

"Understood. Come on." Sunnie pulled me up, and we headed through the emergency back stairwell.

By the fifth flight I asked, "Where are you taking me?"

"You'll see. It's not a secret, but hard to get to."

We reached the seventh floor, the top level of the library, and I prepared to exit the stairwell when she continued to climb. "Where are you going?"

"The roof. Come on."

I hated everything I was doing. There was no adrenaline pumping through my veins, it all just felt stupid. My job was a good job, it wasn't what I envisioned doing with my life, but it still was a good job, better than many of my fellow college students. And sneaking around the Wexler felt like high school pranks.

But I followed her anyway.

There was a small, locked door. Sunnie pulled a wire from her pocket and unlocked it. Inside was pitch black and noisy, like fans and electricity. A constant thump, thump, thump went on like an air conditioner on the brink of its usefulness.

"Careful around the pipes," Sunnie warned me as I tried to navigate in the dark maze. We stopped. I heard something being turned, and then the dusky light from outside came in through a hatchway. She crawled through easily with her little frame. I was not big necessary, very average I'd say, maybe slightly thin, but I couldn't figure how to get out. I went headfirst and shimmied the rest.

There wasn't much to look at with the high buildings by us, but it felt incredible being so high in the fresh air. I did feel like Spiderman right then.

"How did you find this place?" I asked.

Sunnie was sitting now on a little ledge looking over 68th Street. "My brother told me about it. He was here ten years ago, but things don't change around here."

I felt like I was in a comic book, like Daredevil would appear or I'd have to defend off the Joker. "It's really cool. Thanks for bringing me."

"You sure about that?" Sunnie turned to me with a wicked, upturned grin. "I could get you fired."

"No, you couldn't," I replied. "I'm a good employee. Even if I got in trouble, I'd doubt they'd fire me."

"Even with you missing work?"

"How do you know that? Are you stalking me?"

"I'm here a lot," she clarified. "I just noticed you weren't, that's all."

"Anyway," I tried to change the subject. "It doesn't matter. I am graduating, and if I don't head to graduate school, I should start trying to find a new, grown-up job."

"Will you stay in the city?"

"I've never considered leaving, honestly."

She came over and took my hand. "Good, then you can stay with me longer."

Wow, this girl was forward. I had a good time with her last night, until the vomiting episode, but I hardly knew her. She cocked her eyebrow; she might be teasing me. I relaxed, but still wasn't sure.

"Like the view?" she asked. "I sometimes come up here to read. That way I don't have to check out the books."

"Are you against checking books out?"

"I tend to get fines," she answered honestly.

"Do you mostly read vampire fiction?" The question was contrived, but I was curious about how much she knew.

She smiled. "Well, I read other things, like horror or paranormal with a touch of romance, but vampire stuff is my favorite. I like to see what kind of interpretations people come up with in their writing."

I walked over and peered off the ledge. "Do you know a lot about vampires?" I asked, watching the busy street life below. "I mean, like all the folklore like garlic and whatever…" I was baiting her. It was tremendously amusing. I, like everyone else, had a roundabout knowledge of vampire folklore—stakes through the heart, no reflection, garlic, holy water. I also found out it was a lot of bunk, but I hadn't looked into it as others had. I couldn't help but ask.

"I do," she returned enthusiastically.

I immediately feared the conversation I had started.

"It is really amazing how wrong people are about vampires," Sunnie started. "There are so many myths about it. A lot of the traditions started with pagans or catholic priests— that's where a lot of the soulless, holy water, crucifixes stuff came from. But, if you research back in history about vampires in other cultures, you will find some sort of story or folklore about blood drinkers."

"Like what?"

Sunnie grew in animation as she explained. "Like in old Slavic stories, vampires would appear as butterflies symbolizing a departed soul. Isn't that a beautiful idea?"

"Not bad," I admitted, charmed.

"Stories go back as far as Greek and Roman mythology about women feasting on the blood of children."

I laughed. "But that's mythology."

Sunnie pointed up to the sky. "Are you telling me that these stars aren't real?"

"I said nothing about the stars."

"But the stories came from somewhere. They had a thread to something. There are stories in China about blood drinkers back before the birth of Christ and the same story is told in Mesopotamia at the same time without either one's knowledge. It's not like they went on the internet and looked it up like we can. I really believe it came from somewhere."

As much as I wanted to argue, what right had I? I was what she was talking about. Throughout the night she filled me with beautiful, yet horrifying tales of vampires throughout history. I liked listening to her talk about it, the passion and knowledge about something I never would research.

This was something she cared so much about that I had *the* answer to. But I wasn't sure what I should do. I didn't think I had had sufficient time with her to make this kind of secret known. But why shouldn't I? Mitch knew. And it wasn't kept a secret from him. He didn't care, why should she?

I second guessed as I watched her talk. What if it freaked her out? Would I have to do it? Would I have no other choice but to drink her… I suddenly felt sick.

"Are you okay?" Sunnie asked, noticing my anxiety.

"Fine," I swallowed. I looked at my watch. It was a quarter after ten. "Aren't you hungry?"

"I'm getting there," she admitted.

"Let's get you some food," I said as I pulled her up to her feet. This would be a good distraction for my brain to clear. "That is if we can get out of here."

"Easy," Sunnie smiled. "Ground level exit, always unlocked."

"How often do you come here?"

She just smiled her upturned smile and led the way.

14

SECRECT IDENTITY REVEALED

"KNOW THYSELF."

I took Sunnie to the deli down the street. I didn't eat, telling her I still had issues with my stomach, an easy excuse. We talked and walked around campus. I returned her home around one in the morning, before I headed back to my apartment.

Mitch was still there playing a new shooting game he had borrowed from his DT buddies. I sat down with him and played until morning.

Sunday was a blur. I felt completely drained. My body refused to get up. I could feel the lack of nutrients. Sucking on steak wasn't working. My phone buzzed, but I didn't look at it. I wasn't that important. I did need to study for a final on Tuesday, but I didn't care anymore; I tried to care, but just didn't.

When Sunnie called that evening, I invited her over. With Mitch over, my tiny apartment looked like a human lived there, so I only tidied a little. The Cheeto/Dorito mess was good to keep up appearances. Mitch had stayed over, back to playing his video game. I was glad he had stayed. He helped me calm my nerves and be myself.

I quickly made a blood liver shake before she came and tried to down it as fast as I could. It didn't taste good. It wasn't satisfying. It tasted more like metal than anything, but I forced it down to keep my hunger away.

Sunnie buzzed and I let her up. The first thing out of her mouth was, "Wow, you have Borderlands Beyond? I loved the first. Can I play?"

She quickly sat down by Mitch, and they jumped into a conversation about the different weapons compared to the other versions. Mitch eyed me half-way through their conversation. I think he was impressed.

I pulled out the multi-link and we all played for a while.

After we passed an exceptionally hard board, Mitch decided to leave. I knew he just wanted to give us some space. Though I didn't think it was necessary, it was kind of him to do it. I cornered him in the kitchen as he grabbed his stuff.

"She's cool," Mitch whispered. "Did you see her gun down that skorg attack?"

A small laugh came from my mouth. "I was thinking about telling her," I whispered back.

"Her what?"

"You know, about my condition."

Mitch turned toward me all serious and whispered. "I don't care what you do, just as long as Nadia doesn't know."

"What is the big deal?"

"Well, look at her," he pointed over his shoulder to Sunnie who was still playing the game. "She's great and all, but Nadia . . . whoa."

"I don't get it—"

"Nadia is your fantasy girl. She is unbelievable. It stuns me that you haven't tried to go for her. Sunnie's great, but you are a vamp"—I covered his mouth as he said the word—"and she will eventually want more than what you can give her."

He had a point. I hated that stumbling block, the human versus non-human part of our relationship. But I was trying to become human again. And if I told her I was a vampire, she might not like me all human again. So many questions.

Mitch patted me on the shoulder and left.

I went back and sat on the couch, watching Sunnie's character get shot multiple times and die. I think she did it on purpose.

It was silent, all except the game music left of the death scene.

Sunnie turned to face me. "So, I've been thinking."

"That's a good sign," I joked.

"Well, thank you. But really, it has been on my mind for the few days I have known you, and I have to admit something."

I didn't know where she was going, so I shut my mouth and let her continue.

"You are nothing like I expected you to be."

I laughed. "Expected? What did you expect? Am I not living up to your expectations?" I was being facetious, but my humor can sometimes get lost when serious matters come up.

"Sorry, I don't think I'm very good with words today."

She was so easy to tease. "Why? Do I fluster you?"

"Maybe... and shut up," she returned with a slug in the arm. "You're making me forget my point."

I took a deep breath and smiled. "Sorry, what is your point?"

She smiled back hesitantly. "I've been trying to figure out your secret."

"What secret?" I answered as cool as I've ever been.

"Well, your friend Natalie—"

"Nadia," I corrected.

"Yes. Ever since she called you Parker, I've been trying to figure it out."

I tried to hide how uncomfortable I felt. "Sunnie, there is nothing to figure out. I'm no—"

"Wait, let me finish," she interrupted. "Give me a sec. Can you take off your glasses?"

"Why?"

"Umm..." she squirmed. "I'm thinking Clark Kent or something like that."

"Okay," I answered. I slipped off my glasses and looked now at the fuzzy blob in front of me.

She laughed slightly. "Why did I think that would change anything? Sorry."

I laughed too and placed them back on my face.

Sunnie moved around to get comfortable before she spoke again. "I have a confession. And this goes before you even met me, before you asked me out. I did some digging around and found out some things. I'm sorry, but I was just curious."

This changed things. I got very uncomfortable. "Okay?" I answered with a rather iffy question.

"So, let's see where I should start," she began twirling a long strand of hair that had fallen in her face. "I met up with a friend of mine last week, and she talked about you a little, and I was curious."

"Who's your friend?"

"—and I followed some of your friends, but it turns out that the girl Mitch was with on Friday is a friend of this friend of mine."

"Are you talking about Tivoli?" *The Man-eater.*

"Yes, that's the one. So, when I first moved to New York, I took a jazz dance class that was offered on campus. It was just for fun, no credit or anything, but my friend Samantha and I signed up. Our instructor was a girl named Elsie Van Tassel. And she was so good and funny. We became friends and she sometimes invites us down to see her perform. She's a professional dancer and is currently one of the girls in Will Roger's Follies. I went and saw it about three weeks ago and it was so good."

"Elsie?" I questioned. "I don't know an Elsie."

"Are you sure? I think you do. She was the one that told me about you."

"What?" I was more confused than ever.

"She knows I spend a lot of time at the library, and she asked me to check on you. And I'm sorry to be so blunt, but she said that you were just my type. So, when I saw you looking at the vampire fiction I nearly laughed because she said—"

"Elsie?" I asked again.

"—she said you might look at vampire fiction."

My eyes were fidgety as I racked my brain thinking of anyone by that name. It was blank. "And this girl is friends with Tivoli?"

Sunnie became a little bashful. "Yes, she was at the same show I went to. I was going to say something to her on Friday, but I was so nervous."

I was beginning to think I was losing my human memories, when a face flashed before me, a face of a woman I hardly met at the Cell, a dancer who opened my eyes to the hard world of vampirism. "Elcira." I exhaled. "Tall, red-head, very pale."

"Yes!" She jumped on her heals and nearly hugged me.

"Wow. I only met her once."

"She seemed concerned for you for some reason."

But the question came to me: Sunnie was friends with a vampire, does she know that? And this girl, Elcira, mentioned that I was just Sunnie's type. No kidding, the *vampire* type. This might be the answer to my question. I dug deeper.

"Are you concerned?" I asked.

She eyed me curious. "Not really. I have to admit though, you do have some strange habits, but I can deal with those."

"Like what?"

"You're rather a picky eater. I've hardly seen you eat anything."

"I wouldn't worry about that," I tried to smooth it out.

"And are you allergic to the sun? You always smell like coconut sunscreen."

"Uh, yeah," that was a good excuse.

"I know you have allergies to stuff and have a very specific diet. I'm allergic to latex. I get it."

"Wow," I stated as some way to change the subject. I was less impressed with her allergy knowledge. "But what about your friend, Elcira? Elsie, I mean. Do you notice anything about her?" I didn't like this question, but I hadn't the time to figure it out better in my head.

"Well, I don't know," she answered. "Like what?"

"Like what she smells like."

Sunnie sat back and looked at me. "How am I supposed to know that?" She folded her arms.

"I don't know," I backtracked. "I thought maybe we smelled the same, that's all."

"Oh," she softened. "Not that I've noticed. But why would you smell the same?"

"Maybe we shop at the same store." I wasn't covering very well. I just figured all vampires shopped at Vaughn's Ghoulish Emporium.

"Is this about your secret?" Her voice got softer and her eyes intensified. "Elsie has something to do with your secret?"

I scrunched my face and tried not to say anything, but I think my expression gave it away.

"Are you kidding me? What are you telling me? Wait." She stood up and started to pace. "Do you like to dance? Oh no. Are you into theater? Oh, why do I always go for the artsy guys?" She cursed very loudly and mumbled to herself.

At that moment I caught on. I came to her in a rush. "Are you thinking I'm gay?"

She started biting her hand.

"I'm not. Promise. My secret has nothing to do with that. I'm not the theater type. No, no, no. I'm a reader type."

"Then what is it? I've tried to think what it is, and I haven't, and it really bothers me."

"Really, it's not that big of deal, I'm just a vampire, that's all."

Sunnie stood there with a blank expression. "That is so stupid, Ollie."

"No really, feel." I grabbed her hand and placed it on my chest, my vacant heart still not thumping under my ribs.

Sunnie's expression went to an amazed smile and then her eyes glazed over as she fainted on my floor.

15

FREAKING OUT

"TRUE WISDOM COMES TO EACH OF US WHEN WE REALIZE HOW LITTLE WE UNDERSTAND ABOUT LIFE, OURSELVES, AND THE WORLD AROUND US."

And there it was. The truth. And I now had an unconscious girl lying on my living room rug.

I knelt beside her, patting her hand. Her eyes flitted open and she sat up staring at me. She screamed once out of panic before she began to take deep breaths to calm herself.

"Feel better now?" I asked.

"A little, yeah," she responded as she moved over to my couch.

"Do you want a drink?"

"Yes… NO!! Wait, what do you mean?" Her hands went out in front of her for protection.

"Calm down. I'm not going to drink you." I tried to reassure her, while grabbing a glass of water. I can't believe those words came out of my mouth, but they had. When I returned, Sunnie was hugging her knees. "Here," I offered her the drink.

At first, she was reluctant, looking over the water a few times before she took it. "Thanks," she mumbled.

"Are you really nervous?"

She shifted her position a little. "Well, I don't know, kind of."

I tried to get her to relax. Her reaction was what I expected, but I hadn't thought about how to handle it. All the words ran around in my head about what I should say at this moment but getting them out was another matter. "Out of anybody, I figured you would be the most understanding."

She took a long gulp of water and looked back at me. "It's one thing to read about the fantasy, but to know it as reality is a little alarming. I'm sure you understand that."

"Fair enough," I agreed. My brain hadn't nearly forgotten the horror of discovery. The moment grew silent as I tried to act normal while she stared at me with her non-blinking eyes. "Well," I spoke up, "Do you have any questions?"

She slowly nodded. Her fingers went up to my mouth and parted my lips. "No fangs?"

"Not really," I returned, moving around my own teeth with my tongue. They didn't feel different, but I hadn't paid attention.

"Do you feel pain?"

I liked that question. Sunnie surprised me with her intelligence and attention to detail. "I do, but it is different than how I experienced it before."

"Can you cry?"

"I'll just say no to that one," I smiled.

Sunnie's legs began to relax a little, I could tell. She was loosening up with the gentle talk. A cute smile hid in the corner of her mouth. "So, how old are you?"

"Twenty-three," I answered.

"Sorry, I mean, how old are you for a vampire?"

"Ah, I would still be twenty-three."

She looked at me confused. "But how long have you been a vampire?"

"I don't know, about three weeks."

Her expression changed. She looked panicked again. "Three weeks?"

"As of yesterday."

Her hands went back up to her mouth and she screamed a little in her terrified way. "Are you kidding? No kidding?"

"I don't understand what the—"

"You're a newborn?"

"A what?"

"Freshly bitten, fresh to the vampire diet." She began to crumble again.

"Well, I guess so, but I wouldn't classify myself as a newborn." I was clueless why she was shuttering.

"Newborns have an uncontrollable appetite."

"They do? Says who?" I asked. I mean, where was she getting this stuff?

"Stringoi, Lhiannon Shea, the Tale of Mercy Brown, Stephenie Meyer—"

"Whoa," I interrupted. "Are you still afraid I'm going to drink your blood?"

"You won't help yourself," Sunnie said exaggerating her expressions. "You can't control how you feel or how you act."

"Yes, I can," I returned. "I'm just the same. I admit I was upset when I found out, but I haven't been biting people like crazy."

"I probably smell so tantalizing to you right now. You're so brave to be around me—"

She was losing it. "Really, Sunnie, I'm just fine. You smell lovely, I'm sure, for a girl. Whatever you perfume yourself with is just fine. But it's not like I smell your blood and thirst for it. I don't smell anything like that. Well, that's how it is for me anyway."

I know she heard the words, but I don't think she was listening. "How did it happen?"

I sat and relayed to her the most boring details of my morning run.

"That poor girl," escaped her lips.

"What do you mean? I was the one who was attacked."

Sunnie smiled, more relaxed than before. "She doesn't know what happened to her. She's acting out of instinct. That's what I mean by Newborn."

When she put it that way, I did feel bad.

Sunnie sat up, hugging a pillow, and looked at me very matter-of-factly. "Have you killed anyone?"

"Ick. No." It sounded a little wimpier than I wished, but it was a gut reaction. I had no control over how it sounded— like a boy who had been kissed unexpectedly by a girl.

"But how do you..." she trailed off. "How are you surviving if you haven't—"

"Diet," I tried to explain. "My body isn't working right for a vampire. And I don't think it's the newness of the lifestyle or the Newborn whatever-you-were-talking-about. There is seriously something wrong with me. Nadia has taught me a few—"

"Nadia, the restaurant Nadia? That girl?" Her wheels were turning. "Holy, are you kidding? I was eating with vampires that night? Is she a—"

"Yes." I thought she might pass out again, but instead she drank the rest of the water.

"And this is the whole 'Parker' thing, right?"

"Yes."

She stood up and looked at me. "This is crazy." She no longer looked terrified, but more amused. "The restaurant 'Nosferatu' and everything, I was eating with vampires. Was everyone there a vampire?"

"Mitch isn't," I clarified.

"But he knows, doesn't he?"

"Yes."

She pulled her fingernails to her lips. I understood she was nervous, but she was enjoying it. "This is so crazy," she mumbled to herself. "Are all your friends like you?"

I smirked uncomfortably. "I can't say."

"They have killed people," she answered in understanding. "Wait..." a small light bulb turned on. "Tivoli, the one that was with Mitch that night, the one who is friends with Elsie . . ." She trailed off. "Oh no. Do you think Elsie is in danger?"

I smirked. "I think it is more complicated than that."

"Oh no." Her eyes welled up with tears so fast that I had no reaction for it. "She's like you, isn't she?" Her voice was now a whisper.

I nodded with nothing else to say.

"Do you think she's killed...?"

I couldn't lie to her. "I don't know. If I had a guess though, I think all of them have."

She swore again. "What do I do?"

"Sunnie, don't let this change you. This has nothing to do with you."

"Am I safe? Am I on the list of those who will not be dinner?"

"Well," I thought about it. "I couldn't say. Do you really think a list like that exists?"

She wiped her tears and looked away.

I tried to distract her from feeling so lost. "There are a lot of substitutions in place for human blood, but I can tell that all the herbs and animals and synthetic what-have-you will only work for a little while. But there are other ways to get blood. Like the letting clubs and the restaurants."

"But what about you?" she asked tenderly. "Are you a vegetarian like Edward?"

"Who's Edward?"

"If you don't drink human blood, then what? Animals?"

I moved uncomfortably. "I'm a little more complicated than that."

"I'm not understanding."

"I'm allergic."

"To blood?"

"To being a vampire." My exaggeration was a bit dramatic, but in all honesty, that was how I felt. "They don't know what is wrong with me. I should have made the crossover fine. I should be drinking blood like everyone else by now, but I can't." I reached a point of agitation with the entire thing when Sunnie came up to me and grabbed my hand.

"Listen," she looked at her hand in mine. "I hope this doesn't sound dumb, but if you were um... what you said, made the 'Crossover', you wouldn't be here with me. I wouldn't be next to you. I would probably be dead by now."

"I doubt it," I laughed through my anguish. "I still don't think I could hurt anything."

"I'm glad to know this." She let out a long-exhausted sigh and looked up.

Sunnie Knight had very light, beautiful brown eyes centered with green that lit like emeralds when wet from all the tears. I wanted to kiss her. I think I wanted to before but was nervous that I would frighten her. Now that I knew I wouldn't, that she would stay, the time felt right.

I leaned in. I got closer to her very soft-looking mouth.

Sunnie sat in suspension before she sat up, pulling her hand away. "I think I need to be going," she mumbled.

"Is something wrong?" I asked, feeling awkward at her abrupt direction.

"I'm sorry, Oliver," she apologized. "This is a lot to take in for one night."

I smiled in defeat. "I understand."

She grabbed her bag and headed for the door.

"Do you want me to walk you home?"

Sunnie half-smiled as she turned from the door. "Thanks, but I'll be fine. I don't want the truth about vampires to scare me away from loving this city."

"Sunnie," I called back to her. "I'm sorry you know."

"Why?"

"Your world may change." Like mine did.

"You're right. It will," she returned. "And we'll just have to see what happens." She smiled her upturn smile I remembered from the library as she walked away from me.

I knew immediately that I had freaked her out.

16

PHILOSOPHY OR THE LACK THEREOF

"TRUE KNOWLEDGE EXISTS IN KNOWING THAT YOU KNOW NOTHING."

I didn't get any response from Sunnie for two days. I figured as much but hoped she might like to talk to me a little. I called her a bunch of times, but she never answered.

I returned to work on Tuesday and immediately went down to the Juvenile section and grabbed Vampirologist for my own check out. I cracked it open at my computer when I overheard Beth laughing from across the desk.

"What?" I stupidly flipped my hand.

"What are you reading?" she smirked. "Sorry to ask that, but you don't have your usual philosophical study guide by you."

I felt uncomfortable lying, so I did the best I could to cover the truth. "Just looking for something to fill my time."

"Yes, but don't you have a final tomorrow."

She was right. "I forgot."

"Forgot?" she laughed again. "How could you forget? It was all you talked about back in March, because of how poorly you did on them mid-term."

With everything in my un-life right now, my final was the last thing I wanted. Sure, my life felt slightly different now. Was my education really that important now anyway? But this was what I worked up to for the past four years, and for me to waste it because I was *preoccupied* seemed stupid. I immediately went to the school website and logged on to my account, read through some of my class emails that I had ignored, and found information about a study group that was meeting in an hour.

"Do you mind if I leave?" I asked Beth.

She smiled a pretty smile, which made me a little uncomfortable. "Go ahead."

"Thanks," I returned as I packed up my stuff and left. The alarm sounded as I went through the door, but I didn't stop. I forgot I still had Vampirologist in my hand.

This was my last class, the last class for my degree, only offered Spring semester. I often thought of graduate school, I had always liked the idea, but with my lifestyle change, it was the last of my priorities. Even though I had always been a good student from the start, my lack of caring had increased immensely as the end crept closer, and the vampire thing added a thick skin to the layer. I couldn't have been less motivated to go to this study group, but I had been out of the loop for the last three weeks, and my fear of failure came back to haunt me. I better do this right.

The group was meeting off campus in a coffee house called Lampwick's on third. And it might have taken me a while to walk down there, so I rushed. I arrived in plenty of time, but I could see I wasn't the only one here from my class.

"Wow, I never dreamed I'd see you again," the scratchy voice of David Littlelight called to me from his large macchiato. "Thought you had joined the dead," he joked.

"Funny," I tried to laugh back.

David was a free spirit hippie type, beard and all. He took philosophy very seriously and hoped to travel around the world on a train with his guitar, Edna. I remember once him describing his ideal job growing medical marijuana on the California coast.

"No, honestly, you got to tell me where you've been, man," he asked as I sat at his corner table.

"Lot of family stuff going on," I blew it off.

"Hear ya there," he answered like he understood, but I knew he didn't care—his dreadlocks told me that much.

A few others soon joined us, some I had no idea who they were. I had been in the program for years and thought I knew everyone, but maybe I hadn't paid much attention to them before.

We began discussing Martin Heidegger's Being and Time, the points and revelations of his radical thinking of Being. Then the talk ran into Nazis and completely derailed when they began discussing current politics versus Nazi politics.

"Everyone," I tried to steer it back to the topic. "I think you might be judging Heidegger's personal ideas against his theories and slighting your own judgment."

"Yes, but he was a Nazi, and his ideals could slight with the party," replied a girl with giant red curls around her head.

This was going nowhere. Nazi Germany was not a subject I cared to talk about. It was completely irrelevant. "Let's get back to the point of Being."

"I think we covered 'Being' enough in class," the girl glared at me. "If you were there in class, you might understand it better."

I couldn't believe how rude that was. "I thought we were here to study, not gossip about old German politics."

The girl ignored me and turned to the person next to her. "Did you know Hannah Arendt was said to have had an affair with him… and she was Jewish," she continued on about everything I hated.

A reasonable complaint: I ran down here to study, I missed hours at work to be here, I think that counts for a little anger. This wasn't philosophy, this was personal interest drama. I got into Philosophy for the reason of helping people grasp a deeper meaning to life, but what I really learned was I hated intellectualism. Did this girl take the class because she thought it was easy? I felt like she was making fun of what I had worked hard to achieve. I looked over at David Littlelight. He looked uncomfortable with how everything turned. He continued to sip his coffee.

I examined David closer. He possibly set out trying to find meaning in every little nuance in life, a perspective on everything. I think he forgot that we live on Earth and deal with breathing in and out every day.

My own personal light bulb turned on, my own personal revelation—I hated this, all of it. My gut hit the floor as I felt the crushing wave of life barrel down on me. I've been wasting my time caring about something no one should care about. It rocked my core and sent my mind to a black space full of nothing.

Something snapped inside. I devised something so evil, so devilish it surprised me: I wouldn't mind drinking her blood or any of these people. They were vomiting on my passion, and I absolutely hated them.

One less philosophy major in the world. So what? Would anyone really miss them? Would the world be a better place? No one would have to listen to them nitpick every fiber of life down to the intricate workings of your Being.

And David might taste a little funny, I amused myself, flavored with a little something extra.

A bell rang from the cafe door being opened. My brain was caught out of thought. Did someone say my name?

I turned. "Elcira?" I asked, hardly remembering what she looked like.

"What did you tell her?" she immediately came right to the point. The others around me looked in wonder. I quickly grabbed my things and excused myself.

"I don't know what you mean," I returned, though I knew exactly what she meant.

Elcira was fired up, ready to attack. I thought I had seen a vampire's anger or might have an idea of what it looked like—I was mistaken. "What the fucking hell did you tell Sunnie? Did you?"

I quickly walked past her out of the cafe. The sun hung low on the other side of the city as the nightlife started picking up. As typical New Yorkers, everyone outside was too busy with their own lives to worry about our argument.

"Oliver, this is serious," Elcira stated from behind me.

"Why?" I turned. "It really shouldn't be that big of deal. There are others who know—Mitch, Vaughn, Dr. Heck—they know about us, it shouldn't be a big deal. Why not Sunnie? She's the perfect person to know."

Elcira came close with her finger pointed. "Sunnie is innocent and loving. To expose her to this ugly world is unfair. She should never learn the truth. I was trying to protect her."

"I don't get it," I return. "Protect her from what?"

"You are new to this, I'm not," she stated rather sincerely. "There are some pretty horrible people out there. Some that would lure her in and swallow her whole."

"Like me?" I aimed back. "You think I'm dangerous."

"In a way. I don't think *you* know what you are yet, and I think that could be dangerous."

"But you were the one that gave her the idea to come to me."

Elcira walked forward again. I followed. "Yes, but honestly, I didn't think it would get her anywhere. Oh, Oliver, this is such a mess."

"I had to tell her," I said trying to clear my brain. "It just came out. She concluded I had to be gay, with all my bookishness."

Elcira stopped, looked at me and flat out laughed. "Oh, really," she said. "You're really not their type. You wouldn't fit in with them. I wonder if the LGBT community would be flattered to know they are being compared to vampires?"

I returned a smile but didn't answer her question. I honestly didn't know. "So, what do I do?"

"It's more like what do we do?" Elcira returned. "She called me late last night and asked me if it was true. I pretended like I didn't know what she was talking about and then had to rush off the phone."

"I think then," I said as I tried forming a conclusion, "if she is to really understand, we have to both talk to her."

Elcira glanced up at me. "I don't want to do that."

"I don't think you have a choice," I returned with a small smile. "Hey, are you hungry?".

Elcira stopped and looked at me quizzically.

"Have you ever tried Philosophy major?"

She began to laugh. "I'm afraid of what that might taste like."

"Another day then."

She might have thought it was a joke, but I kept it in the back of my mind, just in case.

Elcira sent Sunnie a text message and asked if she could come visit her at her apartment. She replied saying she would be there. I hoped she wouldn't freak out to see me also.

We discussed briefly about what we might say on the way, but nothing really sounded good. I guess it all came down to honesty.

The walk with Elcira felt good. I discovered what a truly delightful person she was, and I hated that I put her in such an uncomfortable spot. I learned about how careful she has been in her vampire life, how guarded she was about relationships, about her twin sister who was currently at Julliard and who also had no idea Elcira was a vampire, and how scared she would be when the truth finally came out.

I apologized again about outing her, if I could use that term.

"You know what," she commented. "It's really okay. It makes me face something I'm scared to do. And really, I need to do this. I hate not being honest with people or having to hide certain aspects of my life from those I love."

As she said that, thoughts drifted to my own family. I was aware of what I needed to do, and I had to do it soon. Waiting for this possible Vampire miracle cure was not the best idea.

If it worked or if it didn't, I didn't think I would ever be 100% myself again. And if I wanted to have my family on my side, I needed to tell them in the right way. "I think I better tell my parents too," I blurted out my thoughts.

"Then let's make a pact." Elcira stopped outside of Sunnie's apartment complex. "I will tell Jocelyn, and you tell your parents, deal?"

"Wow, okay," I shook her hand. "We have a deal."

Elcira smiled, but then took a deep breath. "Alright, let's get this one over with first."

I nodded and we walked in the gated garden area to Sunnie's apartment.

My plan, I would wait outside. Elcira would ask her to come out and then I would walk up, so she wouldn't be so surprised.

Elcira buzzed and was let in.

I just wandered around with my hands in my pockets looking at the spring flowers popping out of the ground. I wasn't sneezing and my eyes hadn't swollen shut. That was a nice feeling. I took a seat on the stone bench near a small coy pond. I waited around ten minutes before the fiery red hair of Elcira came out of the door with Sunnie. I considered walking right to them. I even readied my stride, but I caught a snippet of their conversation and froze.

"...really don't care. I'd just rather you leave," Sunnie said.

"Sunnie, just understand me for a second," Elcira returned.

"I am trying, Elsie, really. And I don't want you to take this personally, but I—" Sunnie grew quiet. "I just don't trust you."

"Do you really think I would hurt you?" Elcira's movements were emphatic, even exaggerated.

"But you kill people." she whispered.

"Not my friends."

Sunnie sat on the porch steps. "Oh, I hate this, and I hate Oliver for telling me."

"This is only confirming what you already figured out before." Elcira sat down next to her. "Let's put this into perspective. Would you like to live in a world where you didn't know that vampires were real and the real danger is out there for you, or would you rather know there are vampires out there and have the comfort of knowing you have friends that will help protect you. We are on your side and there are many that are not."

"I've studied this for so long. I knew I was right but couldn't believe I was right." Sunnie fussed with her hair before speaking again. "So, there *are* bad vampires."

"There are bad *people* out there," Elcira stated. She had such compassion behind her words. "There are a lot more *bad people* that want to hurt or destroy everything, more than there are vampires wanting to suck you dry."

"I know you're right. It's just so horrifying."

"I think you read too much. It's not like all those novels."

Sunnie laughed a little. "Maybe."

"Just imagine how we feel. Like poor Oliver was just on a morning jog when he was attacked." My stomach dropped at the sound of my name. "And now he can't even drink blood."

"What? Really?"

I hated them discussing me like I was this wussy vampire.

"He didn't tell you that?"

"Honestly, if he mentioned it, I probably missed it anyway, I was in such shock."

"Good point."

"Ah, geez," Sunnie huffed as her head sunk into her hands. "I never thought about that. I didn't even consider his feelings.

Does he still have those? I feel so bad now. I haven't talked to him or anything since he told me."

I watched Elcira's head crane around looking for me. "I think you should talk to him," she caught my eye back in the shadows of the garden. Sunnie didn't see it.

"You are right," she said as she pulled out her phone and dialed my number.

Immediately my phone went off playing some Lady Gaga song that I didn't know. Mitch must have got a hold of my phone…again and changed my ringtone… again. I tried to silence it as fast as I could as I fumbled around, sneaking behind the bench and out of sight. I could see her attention turn toward the garden, but I don't think she could see me when I answered.

"Hello. Ahem . . . sorry." I cleared my throat and started to whisper. "Hello?"

"Oliver?"

"Yes... sorry, yes this is me. Oliver, yes. Sunnie?"

"Yes, it's me. Where are you? Are you okay? You sound like you are in trouble?"

"No, I'm just fine thanks," I still spoke in hushed tones.

"There is so much I want to say to you. First, I really am so—"

"Ah. Great!"

"But you didn't let me—"

"Really. Oh, thanks." Honestly, I hadn't heard a word of what she was saying, I was about to fall like a potato bug on my back.

"Oliver, seriously, is something going on?"

"No, shush. Really . . . fine . . ."

"Ollie. I wanted to—" she stopped.

A siren rushed by echoing in my phone.

I watched her head move around. Her tone switched. "Ollie, where are you?"

"I was just heading down your way," I returned in a hurry.

"Why?"

"To see you."

I watched her move her head around and spot me. I felt like the stupidest person in the world, crouching behind that bench. She stood up, phone in hand, and walked to where I was. I looked up to see her face, confused and stern, looking directly into my eyes.

"Need something?" she said straight-faced with a little attitude.

"Ah. Hi." I sighed as I stood up.

"What the hell, Oliver?" I think she couldn't think of anything else to say.

"I came with Elcira," I admitted sheepishly. "I thought she would have told you I was here."

"But why did you think you needed to hide?"

"I didn't at first. I started that way and then you were talking about me, and I felt awkward. So, I moved back and then you called and… and… that's all." I heaved.

"Oliver." Sunnie shook her head. "I'm sorry."

"Wait, you are?"

"Of course," she said as she moved her eyes away from me. "I might need some time, but I didn't know how to say it, so I just didn't say anything and avoided it all together."

"I'm embarrassed I told you. I ruined everything."

"Don't be," she smiled back at me, her bright eyes hit me hard. "I like it. It makes you more . . . I don't know . . . more mysterious, dangerous maybe. It's a little fun."

"Yes," I agreed, "but it also makes me a little complicated too."

Sunnie turned her head to the side. "Well, I read 'Twilight' and I'm sure that it can't be much harder than that."

"I don't know what you are talking about, but I don't think you should follow the advice of a vampire romance on this."

She smirked. "I know that, but it does provide tips." Her eyes were smiling, and at the moment I didn't care that she liked reading silly teen vampire romance for tips.

I leaned in and kissed her. I could tell she was tentative. I thought it felt pretty good, until she pulled back and smacked me in the face.

"Do you feel that?" she asked sincerely.

"Oh course," I returned rubbing my cheek.

"Sorry," and then she leaned in again and kissed me back. I think I'd forgiven her.

17

A PRAGMATIC PRINCIPLE

"FALSE WORDS ARE NOT ONLY EVIL IN THEMSELVES, BUT THEY INFECT THE SOUL WITH EVIL."

My phone rang again. It was the same obnoxious song that played before. I broke from Sunnie, embarrassed.

"I didn't figure you liked that kind of music," Sunnie said.

"Some funny joke, eh?" I blew it off.

It was Nadia, and that was a surprise. I felt awkward thinking of her next to Sunnie.

"Hello?" I answer.

"Hey, Parker, still hate me?" was the first thing she said.

"I never considered that an option," I tried to joke.

"We still on for tomorrow night?"

Tomorrow night? What was tomorrow night? Had I planned something? Oh, wait. "My transfusion?"

"Good, you remembered," she returned in the phone. "Mitch bet me money you would forget. So, I have to thank you for the twenty."

"Ah, sure," I replied uncomfortable. She gave more instructions and hung up.

I looked over at Sunnie, who had a very concerned look on her face. "Transfusion?"

Elcira had given us a little privacy, but when my phone rang, she came over for the conversation. "Was that Nadia?"

I told them both that I needed to meet with her and Andrus up at Dr. Lennox's Blood Bank for another experiment.

"What do you mean *experiment*?" Sunnie asked.

"They are trying to fix me," I explained without explaining.

"Because you are a broken vampire?"

"Yes," I answered, withholding the truth that I hoped to be fixed from being a halfway vampire to not a vampire at all.

"Well, I want to come," Sunnie asked.

Both Elcira and I yelled, "No!"

"Why?"

"Lennox would eat you alive," Elcira said off hand. It was a light comment that turned Sunnie's face green.

"Because Lennox is a real vampire, not like me," I tried to explain.

Elcira looked a little sad. "He is one of the scariest around. Little children, Halloween night kind of scary. I mean, he drains bodies of the dead as part of his hospital duties."

I squirmed a little at that.

"If Lennox is there, I can't let you go," I reiterated.

"Fine, but if he isn't, I'm there, got it?"

No problem. Lennox would be there.

Next day was my final, and this was tricky. It was at nine in the morning, actually in the Hunter College Testing Center, and I had to prepare to be outside.

It was projected to be around 90 degrees. Of course, it couldn't be a rainy day in New York. Not with my luck.

I showered thoroughly and lathered up with the few products I had to help reduce my smell and protect my skin in the sunlight. I also dressed protectively. I gathered up my black hoodie Nadia gave me from VO and pulled the hood high to cover my face well. I considered taking an umbrella for more sun protection but thought it might be a little too much. I shoved my bare hands into my pants pockets.

The walk to campus was hard. I hadn't experienced such a wonderful sun in a long time, and it kept me barreling in alleyways and umbrella shade the entire way.

I got into the testing center, scanned, signed in, and started the stupidest test I have ever taken.

Here's the thing about Philosophy, if you hadn't guessed it. The answers to questions asked are completely subjective to a point of view. Every conclusion made could be construed to fit your own personal opinion and ideals. The thing you need to practice in Philosophy is how to get the other side to believe your argument and trust that you believe it too.

Professor Martin was a little trickier than most. She believed anyone, and your argument needed to form with her own opinion in order for you to be right. I had never been one for persuasive argument, that's why I got in Philosophy in the first place and not Public Relations.

Many of the questions were essay questions, which I hated. What was she doing? Playing a game with our brains? I no longer cared about the Pragmatic Principle. I figured if I turned the question inside out, it might help me. Instead of talking about Pierce's Conception of Practical Objects, I mixed it around to objects that conceive practicality. It looked like it worked for a moment before I figured Martin would see through it.

But really, what was wrong with me? Maybe the vampire in my body now had killed off all understanding in Philosophy. I have been studying this stuff for the last four years. Hunter had a great program for it. I shouldn't worry about it so much. It should come naturally.

I breezed through the True and False and guessed half-heartedly at the multiple-choice section.

Then the last question:

Discuss Husserl's Intentionality and how you, personally, experience this?

I admitted, I was smarmy, but I was done with this test all together.

"Everything in my conscious has been thrown and mixed into a bag of unrealistic reality. If you observe that I do things out of habit, I admit that I do and if that is my intention, who give a flying fig about it. And for my personal experience, I personally experience violent illness when I think of this class and of Philosophy in general, and consciously restrain myself every second from vomiting all over this test."

I saved it, clicked out, and left my life in Philosophy behind.

Was I disappointed? Sure. I might not graduate right now. It happens. All those years wasted. I never wanted to discuss anything philosophical again. Nadia could tell I was upset when she arrived at my house at nine.

"You okay?" she asked. It was nice to have a sincere concern from her.

"I'll be fine," I smirked. "I don't know what I'm going to do if I don't graduate."

Nadia grinned. "Well, what would you do if you did?"

That was a very good question that I had no response to.

"Thing is, Park," Nadia turned back to me, "you have a new life ahead of you. Maybe you should look at what you could do with that."

"But if I change back to a—"

"We'll try. No guarantees." Nadia nearly pushed me out the door. "But that's not the point. What do you do with a Philosophy degree? *Do you want fries with that?'* I know you want to influence people, but nobody wants to hear what philosophers have to say."

This was a bit tough to swallow, but I think she had a point. When Krysztof first met me, he didn't know what to do with a philosopher vampire. Good point, I wouldn't know either.

Nadia nudged me on the shoulder. "I wouldn't worry about it, Oliver. I promise, you will make the right decision."

"Thanks," I muttered, a little defeated.

"Are you ready?"

"I guess so. Will Lennox be there?"

"No, just Andrus, Elle, and me. We figured it would be best to keep Lennox out of this. He's gone away to a conference in France, so right now is the perfect time to experiment."

The words hit me like a ton of bricks. "Can we make a stop before we go," I said?

"Why?"

"I made a stupid promise."

Twenty minutes later, I sat in the back of the cab in between two very upset women—Nadia and Sunnie. I didn't think it would be a big deal. Nadia absolutely hated the idea of grabbing Sunnie, but I made a promise. Yes, I guess I didn't need to tell her, but if I didn't, she would find out some way. I thought I'd play it safe. When Sunnie found out I was going with Nadia, things turned weird.

Women can be so strange sometimes.

I felt awkward sitting between them. Neither talked. The atmosphere filled thick with intense feminine stubbornness. I tried to lighten up things with gentle conversation.

"I read that Vampirologist book, and I think it is completely inaccurate."

"It's meant for kids, Park," Nadia returned rather smug.

"Well, it might be," Sunnie replied. "But there are some very interesting facts in there, sources you can't find other places."

"Sources? What sources?" Nadia turned toward her. "And how many would you know, sweetheart?"

"I didn't mean it as an explanation, but something to gear others in a direction that is not typical to vampire novels."

"What it is, is just a way to catch the vampire hype and frighten children at night."

"Are you telling me that you don't want to scare children?"

Well, that was a bad idea. They argued for the rest of the ride. It wasn't much of a fight, but a strong differing of opinion. I didn't think Nadia knew anything about Vampire fiction, and Sunnie knew nothing about Vampire reality. The point was futile on both sides. I sighed in relief when the hospital came in focus around the trees.

Andrus met us at the door and got us through security. He looked rather surprised to see Sunnie but got her through.

Closer to the blood bank he turned to Nadia. I overheard them exchange some worried words. Now I felt bad about bringing her.

"Sunnie?" I grabbed her arm and slowed down. I hadn't noticed how pale she had become. "Are you okay?"

She slowly nodded. "I'm just a little squeamish, that's all."

"Well, then why did you insist on coming?"

"I wanted to be supportive."

An endearing sentiment, but completely ridiculous. I took her hand to help her out. She clung on so tight it might have hurt if I were human. When we entered the infusion room, Sunnie's eyes grew wide, right before she passed out onto the floor.

18

NANA'S BLOOD PUDDING

"BE SLOW TO FALL INTO FRIENDSHIP; BUT
WHEN THOU ART IN, CONTINUE FIRM AND
CONSTANT."

Sunnie's eyes flitted open a few minutes later. She turned and promptly threw up several times. Andrus took her to a different room to help her recover while we finished my transfusion.

The red cell exchange transfusion felt strange, pulling, flushing, and replacing all the sludgy crud in my veins. It wasn't as nasty as before, but still felt unnatural and unpleasant. The ghost sensation remained in my veins, like the blood wanted to course through my system, ever so slight, numbing my chest around my heart.

Nadia stayed by me the entire time and kept me company. It was good to talk again. I really had missed her company. Ever since I had become a vampire, she had been there to help me, save me actually. I remembered what Mitch had said when he compared Sunnie to Nadia. I didn't think that mattered much anymore, since Sunnie had an interest in me too. I didn't think Nadia would ever consider me more than that poor, pathetic soul who needed a hand. However, I watched her taking such interest in my case, my idea of her was also changing. Such a stunning girl. Could she really be interested in me?

"So, have you worn your dress yet?" I asked, out of the blue. The memory of that dress Vaughn Ohlstrom made stuck out in my mind for some obvious reason.

"My dress?" Nadia's eyebrow lifted. "Oh, no, not yet. The VO Benefit Gala is next week. There should be a lot of prominent VO people, many WVPs."

"Sorry, what is a WVP?" I asked, remembering Elle mention it with my case study.

"Working Vampire Professionals. It would really be something if you came."

"I'm not a professional."

"Who cares. Vaughn would love to have you there."

"Are you inviting me?"

Her eyes met mine in a playful way. "Yes, but vampires only. Understand?"

"I got it," I returned.

"No offense, Park," Nadia said as she finished bandaging me up. "I don't think your girl has the stomach for it," she nudged toward the other room.

I grimaced knowing exactly what she meant. "I thought she might after everything she's read."

Nadia smiled again. I thought she took pleasure in Sunnie's misery. "All patched up," she finished wrapping my arm with some bright green spongy tape. "Not that you really need this, but I want that blood to stay in there."

"What's next for me?"

"Well, we hope to have stripped off any remaining Sulfa out of your system. Its usefulness is done by now. By Monday we hope to have our hands on a drug from Spain called Hemolathitor which might hopefully stimulate your heart muscles and then we are going to try a defibrillator. Sound like fun?"

I looked nervous I was sure, but I laughed with her. "I will never understand your version of fun."

She smirked. "I can be very persuasive."

Sunnie and Andrus came back into the room.

"He's finished," Nadia told them, the funness disappearing right out of her again.

Sunnie looked poor but smiled. "Can I go home now?" she asked weakly.

"Sure," I answered, and we left.

I took Sunnie home. Nadia, Andrus, and Elle had things to discuss about me. The cab ride was enjoyable without the tense awkwardness between the two women.

When I reached Sunnie's apartment, I lifted her up and carried her in. She talked very little, only in brief, fluffy sentences.

I laid Sunnie down on her bed and pulled a blanket over her. She fussed around with her pillow for a moment as I sat on the edge of the bed, watching her and thinking.

"Are you okay?" I asked.

"Of course," she returned, barely awake. "It's just the sedative that Dr. Andrus gave me."

"I just want to make sure," I returned. "It's been a few hard days."

She smiled weakly. "I'll be fine. Just adjusting."

I sat there for a few moments longer. "Can I ask you something?"

She nodded with her eyes closed.

"I have a family party this Saturday in Jersey. Would you like to go with me?"

"You serious?" she mumbled into her pillow.

"Of course. It's my grandmother's eightieth birthday. I was debating whether I should go, but I think I should."

She half-smiled. "Yeah," she returned.

I got up to go. "I'll ask you again tomorrow. You may not remember our conversation."

I thought she was out before I finished my sentence.

Saturday came rather quickly. I achieved practically nothing the last few days. I read a little, worked a little, and finished a few things for my college classes. I also looked through all the details preparing for my graduation; the walk of the graduates, my head and gown size, other information like that. I also received a nasty email from Professor Martin about my test.

"*...I really thought you would take this more seriously... Not impressed with the attitude so arbitrarily displayed... I thought you better... reviewing your case with the other professors and Dean Fessinger, the Head of the Department of Philosophy... seriousness of this behavior...*"

Great. So, now I may not graduate. I sort of cared but wished I didn't. It just is not in my nature to blow something that big. But, if I didn't graduate, what would that mean? I'd have to take the class again next spring. They wouldn't kick me out, would they?

Sunnie tried to get over the vampire thing—her respectful attitude showed it. She came over a few times and helped me with my diet, watched that I didn't intake anything that I might react badly to. She also met me in the library and educated me more on vampire folklore and stigmas that follow the vampire culture.

When Saturday arrived, I felt happy to get out of town, even to visit my folks. It turned out to be an overcast day, which was perfect. I didn't want to hide inside or wear my Hot Topic Bomber Jacket all day in the hot sun.

Mitch, at the last moment, decided he wanted to come. That was fine, we would be fine with three, and Mitch had access to a car, borrowed from a DT Buddy who owed him a favor after a poker game.

I wished to leave early, but I had to run on Mitch time. He finally called at 10:30 a.m. to tell me he was running late. I appreciated the courtesy call, which was unnecessary. I finally heard the honk outside my window and ran downstairs only to find someone else waiting for me.

"Hey," Nadia said with a smile. "Are you going somewhere?" She suddenly saw Mitch in the alleyway in a bright red convertible. "Wow, is this yours?"

Mitch grinned. "No, I wish, but mine for the day."

"Where are you headed?" she asked.

"Ah, Ollie and I are going down to Hopatcong for his grandma's birthday. You should come."

I bit my knuckle.

"Is that where you're from?" Nadia turned to me.

I was flustered. "Ah, yeah," I responded as I ran my fingers through my hair. I didn't mind Nadia coming, I actually preferred her company to Mitch any day, but how was this going to sit with Sunnie?

"No kidding? Hopatcong? It's so beautiful down there. When you said you were from New Jersey, I was thinking Hoboken or Jersey Shore, something like that. I'd love to come."

Umm… What just happened? She can't come. I invited Sunnie. I had to be honest. I needed to be honest. "Are you sure?" I asked again, hoping maybe it would sway her to change her mind. "Boring relatives. Jell-O. You know."

"Ollie, I did come to talk to you about some things, so we might be able to on the way."

"Well, that would be good, but—" I started, then Mitch slowly walked behind her and made some strange face suggesting choking and a big "NO" on his lips.

"Oh," Nadia returned, feeling the intrusion. "Sorry, is there someone else you're bringing?"

"Oh no, I just…" I answered in my haste. Mitch was simulating hanging from a noose. "No, it's fine. I was…n't bringing anyone else." A big, mouthy grin covered my face.

And there started the downfall of my relationships with humans.

I felt awful. I finally mentioned something to Mitch, trying as I could in the back seat of a cherry mustang convertible. Nadia's hair kept whipping me in the face, falling sometimes in my mouth as I spoke. She tried to keep it pinned, but Mitch was a maniac when it came to driving.

The drive, which normally would take an hour and a half was closer to forty-five minutes, and by the time it was over I was glad of it. My insides were being eaten away by guilt. I felt I had better call Sunnie and explain what happened, but then I chickened out when Nadia said something to me.

"Oliver? You grew up here?"

I looked around. Yep, the quiet, sleepy township that Mitch and I terrorized still seemed as sleepy as ever. The lake looked choppy from the wind, but still classic, straight from a postcard painting, fresh with blossoming cherry trees and red maples. It was perfect—way too perfect.

"My parents live over the bridge on the other side."

"This is charming," she said sweetly. "Wait, is this road called the River Styx?"

Mitch and I both started laughing. "Yes," Mitch returned. "Kind of appropriate when you return to Hell."

"Now, how could this be Hell?" Nadia returned.

"You have yet to meet my parents," I commented again. "This town represents failure."

"And why is that?" Nadia asked.

"I didn't become who my parents sought for in a son here."

"And you definitely won't be what they want now either," Mitch remarked off-handedly.

"Wow, he's right," I slumped back down in my seat as we approached nearer and nearer to the lakeside. "I came so I could tell my parents what happened." I couldn't help the hurt and disappointment I felt.

Nadia turned. Her eyes hit mine for a moment then went back to the town. I think she understood the pain I was about to cause, not only that, but the humiliation of the explanation would bother me long after this.

The Brixby home sat on the edge of the lake, a small, quaint little house compared to the grandeur of the lakeside homes across the bridge. It was white and simple, with little gables and old white siding that desperately needed a paint job. I promised my dad that I would help him this summer to paint it. It would have happened last summer, but my mother wanted this awful greenish teal color, which we talked her out of thankfully. The long drive up the gravel driveway took forever or maybe it was my fear that made it seem so long.

Spring had definitely arrived. My mother kept an immaculate garden, already clean of any weeds, revealing blossoms of what looked like hundreds of flowers filling the lakeside of my home. She had gotten worse since I left for school, not caring as much about my allergies.

And there was my mother right in the middle of them all, wearing her worst flower apron and accompanying sun hat, rubber boots, and pink handled spade. She waved us over as we drove up and, realizing it was me, trotted excitedly to the car.

"Boys. You're here," she said out of breath. "Well, I'll tell you, I didn't think you would come. Been threatening rain all today. Hope it doesn't ruin the party. But so glad you made it." She reached over the seat and gave me a dirty kiss on the cheek. "Are you feeling okay, Oliver? You look frightfully pale."

I smiled. "Just the car ride, Mom."

It wasn't until then did she notice Nadia in the passenger seat. "Well, my heavens, sorry about the state I'm in, I'm Shirley Brixby." She quickly took off a garden glove and stuck out her hand, which Nadia gladly accepted.

"Nadia Flematakis," she returned. "I'm a friend of Oliver's."

"That's such a beautiful name. I love names, you know," she continued to ramble, with Nadia paying sweet attention to her like a good girl. I decided to get out of the car and head to the house.

Inside nothing had changed. The kitchen door still squeaked on the hinge, an alarm if anyone entered the house. It still smelled of pancakes and old books like it always had.

The old butcher block table stood in the middle of the room cluttered with freshly cut flowers and other arrangements my mother was making for the party.

I traveled to the living room to find my father in the same place he had been in for the last twenty-two years, sitting in his brown recliner watching ESPN and scribbling in his play book.

"Well, Oliver," he said my name rather slowly. It sounded like I was in trouble. He looked up from his notebook and smiled. "Glad to see you. How are you?"

"Good," I returned, which wasn't far from the truth, very glad to be home.

"Well, sit down son, I've got some plays for you."

My father, Bill Brixby, was the Hopatcong High School basketball coach. I always felt like such a disappointment to him, since I was the worst athlete in the history of the sport of basketball. But my dad learned early on that I had no talent. He supported me in the other things I did, like creative writing. He thought he'd have a better chance with his grandchildren than me. I sighed at the idea and sat next to him on the couch as he showed me some new strategies he was working on.

Within a few minutes my mother came in with Mitch and Nadia. They were laughing as my mother recalled some embarrassing moments of my youth. Ordinarily it would bother me, but for some reason I liked hearing the laughter.

"…but then Oliver looked at the pile of fallen booster seats and put his hands on his hips and said, 'They don't make them like they used to,' and everyone around us started laughing. He was only four years old and such a little man."

Nadia's laugh was charming. I liked hearing it.

"Would you all like something to eat?" my mother asked. I was afraid to answer. "I know the party is in a few hours, but you can snack on whatever you find. Oliver is such a picky eater that he just sometimes has to fend for himself, but anything in here is yours, and don't hesitate to help yourself."

That was my mother, always the hostess. She came over to the living room and gave me another big hug. "Good to see you," she said again and then she whispered, "She's a beauty," in my ear.

I felt bad at my mother's reaction and then thought about Sunnie again. Dread hit my stomach like a ton of bricks.

In the few hours before my Grandma's birthday party, we helped my mother set up tables, arrange decorations, and fix food. My Aunt Margaret came over with my teenage cousins, Paul and Cherie, and she brought my Nana also.

My Nana Bea was one of the craziest, sweetest things on this planet. She fell in love with my grandfather, an American soldier in England, married and moved to the states. After all these years she's never lost her harsh gutter accent.

"Ollie," she hailed as she entered the kitchen where I was slicing watermelon. She came and gave me a sweet kiss on the cheek and smiled. "You got a lovely lady out there."

"Oh, Nadia?" I answered dumbly. "We are just friends, Nana."

"Oh, pish-posh," she grabbed my cheeks together to get a better look at her. Her accent went right through me. "I know you. When 'ave you brought home a girl? I only remember the redhead with the crooked face."

"Honest, Nana, she just appeared on my doorstep," I returned. "And that was Susie Lapinkski, I was fourteen, and she had a flat tire and needed to call home."

"Well, this one's fantastic." She hurried and grabbed a piece of watermelon and stuffed it in her mouth. "I like 'er much better than that redhead. How long 'ave you been seeing 'er?"

It was hard to decipher between the watermelon and the accent what she said. "About a month," I answered honestly. "And we aren't really dating, Nana. Just friends. There is a girl, but she is back in New York."

"And why not bring 'er?"

"I don't know," I returned pathetically, and there again pinched the sting. I probably should contact Sunnie, and yet, I hadn't.

Nana Bea smiled again and grabbed another piece. "Ollie, there is something wrong with you if you don't notice that stunning creature outside. Fantastic girl!" And she went toward the front room.

Something wrong with me? Yes, but much worse than Nana knew. I glanced back outside and watched Nadia helping my mother hang lights around trees by the dock on the lake. I liked her, sure, I mean, I really liked her, but I never figured I should like her as anything other than a friend. She was attractive. I never missed that. Funny and spirited, yes. Nadia was a seductive vampiress. I was Oliver Brixby—Allergy Magnet, Philosophy Failure, and a vampire who can't tolerate blood. I was the saddest excuse of any vampire in the history of vampires. Sunnie was sweet and cute, more what I was used to when dating, more my speed. Right? I couldn't catch Nadia. She was fast-paced and fashionable and funny. What would she ever see in someone like me?

Yet when I looked at her helping my mom, talking with her about who knows what, I got a glimpse of something that could've started my heart. She understood me: my pain and sadness. This vivacious creature had the same curse as me. She would never have children, and it made me feel sorry. Her normal life had radically changed. Did she have family around? I hadn't got to know her well enough to ask. Then I felt like an idiot for never bothering to know.

She caught my eye through the window and winked.

Dammit. That complicated things.

People started arriving around 4:00 p.m.—lots of family that I hadn't seen in a really long time. Manhattan consumed my life, and I was always too busy to come to any function my family put together. We were multiplying; the number of people grew extreme. It felt that anyone who had ever encountered my grandmother was there—old school mates, maybe Nana's old boyfriend, cousins of cousins related on my mother's side, grandkids of cousins. The volume of bodies grew overwhelming. My anxiety of crowds hadn't disappeared. I smiled through it.

The sun peeked in and out of clouds every once in a while. Nadia and I stayed indoors until the sun had fallen passed the tree line and the twinkly lights from the strung Chinese lanterns started reflecting on the water.

My hunger was coming, and Nadia rummaged through the refrigerator for something to satisfy.

"What's this?" Nadia pulled out a Tupperware container with masking tape over the top. It read "Pudding".

"My Nana's pudding, you don't want it, trust me," I said without thought.

Nadia lifted the lid and smelled deep. "Honestly," she sniffed again. "This smells really good. What's in it?"

"It's an old recipe my Nana brought over from England. She always makes it, but no one ever eats it but her. I always felt bad about that, but when I was little, my mother forced me to eat it and thought I might throw-up."

Nadia was very sneaky, but I never saw her so interested in something. "You smell this," she pushed it toward me.

I smelled, and then I smelled it again to make sure my nose wasn't playing tricks. It was blood. I couldn't believe I recognized it. "Blood pudding," I said without thinking.

"And what else, do you think?" she said grabbing a spoon.

"I wouldn't risk it. You might heave."

Nadia's wicked smile returned. I've seen that smile before, the adventurous smile from that night at the Cell. She sought to push me to be adventurous, even though I consider myself boring. Her head nodded toward me, and she took a spoonful.

And she was fine. "Come on, Park, taste it," she made for another spoonful.

I couldn't imagine it tasting better than what I remembered, but my taste buds had changed. I took the spoonful and swallowed. The smell, the aroma, the iron and salt, mixed with the sausage and sweet currants. I took another taste.

"To be honest," I said with a mouthful, "I don't think my Nana is very good at making this. I think there is too much blood in it."

"Lucky for us then," Nadia returned.

My mother swung open the door. "Come out you two," she called. "We are about to light the cake." She looked at me with my spoon in hand and asked, "What are you eating, Oliver?"

"Nana's pudding," I answered.

"It's delicious," Nadia smiled.

My mother brightened. "Well, I'll tell her that," and walked back out the screen door.

"You really have a terrific family, Ollie," Nadia smiled at me.

I placed the lid back on the container and set it back in the fridge. "Thanks, I think so," I returned, walking back outside.

As I stood up and closed the door, I hadn't noticed how dark it had become with the falling light. But I could see Nadia, standing in silhouette looking at me.

It was an impulse reaction, a gnawing in my gut that took over my thoughts and feelings. It was dark. Things could happen in the dark that couldn't happen in the light. I had no plan in my brain for mistakes or repercussions—I stretched forward and kissed her right on the mouth.

The yielding and then the acceptance was both surprising and alarming. Within the kiss I came a little to my senses and pulled back.

I couldn't think of anything to say, so I just whispered to myself, "Okay." Then marched down to the pier past the lights and the cake and the singing and jumped directly into the lake.

19

COMING OUT

"IN CHILDHOOD BE MODEST, IN YOUTH TEMPERATE, IN ADULTHOOD JUST, AND IN OLD AGE PRUDENT."

The water was nice and cold. It helped me wake up from the reality of the moment. *I am an idiot*, I kept saying in my head. I can't believe I just did that.

The splash of the water alerted some of the guests. My mother specifically came rushing over. "Oliver!" she shouted as she ran up the pier. "Oliver! Are you okay?"

I floated on my back in the cool water thinking it should be colder than it felt. "No worries, Mom," I yelled back. "Just trying to come to my senses."

My mother was now at the edge of the pier with a handful of other people, Mitch and Nadia included.

"You about gave me a heart attack."

"I'm fine, really."

Mitch leaned down to me. "Dude, you okay?"

I didn't know what to say with Nadia there, but I blew it off. "Just felt like a swim."

The crowd started to disperse away back to the cake. Nadia caught my eye. I wished I could disappear.

Then she did something I didn't expect—she jumped in.

Mitch was a little confused. He leaned over and splashed his hand in. "Man, you guys are crazy. It's freezing."

"Not really," Nadia surfaced and looked as stunning as ever in the half light at dusk.

Mitch laughed at us and sent a splash my way before returning to the party.

A few moments of quiet night passed between Nadia and me. I felt awkward as I'm sure she did; the sounds of crickets chirping and gentle splashing against the pier soothed my nerves, and I filled with memories of my childhood. It was peaceful.

"Oliver?" Nadia nearly whispered breaking the silence of the night. "Thank you."

"What?" I felt stupid for saying it. It came out of my mouth before I could stop it.

She swam closer to me and treaded in a silent paddle. "I feel bad for making you uncomfortable. I didn't mean to sabotage your evening. You could've brought anyone. But I'm very glad I came," she drifted off for a moment. "It was a sweet moment, and I wanted to thank you."

"Really?"

"You are so fascinating," she might have laughed. "I find you great company."

Great company? I think this was my clue that she didn't really like the kiss. "Are you putting me in the Friend Zone?"

Nadia looked stunned. "Did it come out that way?"

"A little," I returned.

"No. That was not what I meant at all," she tried to clarify. "But I know there is someone else you prefer, so I'm backing away from it."

"Well, I wouldn't say prefer—"

"I'm making this easy for you. You know I don't like human relationships because I've been there, and it leads to bad things all around. But I don't think my opinion on it should be in the way of your happiness. So, I'm just going to stand back. If what Elle and I are trying works, you won't even need to worry about it and can go on dating any human you like. But regardless, I shouldn't force the choice." She ended with a huff. I think she had exhausted her words on me.

I mulled over what she said, chewing them over in my brain. "So, you do like me?" I tried to clarify.

She moved very close and kissed my cheek. "I'll be around."

What was up with girls and code? "Is that a yes?"

She smiled and swam to the shore. I followed.

When we reached the bank, I pulled myself out and lay out on the grass. Nadia soon followed and found a few towels my mother had brought from the house. She mechanically started drying out her hair.

"You are very lucky," she remarked. "I would have killed to have grown up here."

My mind rolled around what she had said. I guess I did take it for granted. "Where did you grow up?"

Her smile faded a little. "I don't like to volunteer information, remember?"

"But are you from Texas?" I asked, remembering a small conversation about her, the only real information I had.

"Actually, no," she returned. "I'm from California, Los Angeles originally, and my family is still there. They were informed of my death long ago, but it wouldn't really matter to them if I lived."

"Why would you say that?" I questioned.

"My parents divorced when I was eight. I lived with my mother. My father hated me. Said it many times that he wished I would forget him. I ran away several times. I got my first tattoo when I was fourteen. I joined the Army to get away from it."

I wished I hadn't asked. "But tell me good things about growing up."

She smiled in a bizarre way. "Well, I really miss chocolate and warm summer beaches. I used to spend every summer down by Marina Del Rey selling stupid looking jewelry my mother made, but when she wasn't around, I would sell whatever in the morning then pocket a few bucks, buy me a big hot dog from a cart my friend Donnie worked at and would just swim the rest of the day. It was really fun."

That did sound fun. I began reflecting on my own life. "Hopatcong is stifling. Things never change. Things never progress. I was always a failure to my father and the community who had hopes for me. I just wanted to run away, but never did until I went to New York—close, but far enough away."

"You are going to tell them, aren't you?" Nadia quieted down.

Ah crap, that awful feeling came back, the one that started in my stomach and worked around to my chest. "Yes," I returned. "After the party."

"Well, I'll be here if you need me," she stood up and went over to where the party was.

I lay back down and tried to plan what I should say to my loving parents.

After a while I still felt pretty soggy, so I went inside to change my clothes. Down in the bottom of my closet, I found some old jeans and a beat-up t-shirt I got from some scholastic competition I hardly remembered. I had forgotten how much I loved those baggy pair of jeans my mother hated. It felt good to wear them again.

I returned to the party and enjoyed myself. A lot of old stories were told around the tables; several of my cousins I didn't know very well had some pretty funny stories of adventures at my Nana's home. I had never been very adventurous and didn't have the same wiles as the other string of DNA had.

Mitch left for a while to visit his folks, taking Nadia with him. I considered joining them, but my nerves would not settle, and I stayed there to deal with the monster before me.

Around nine, groups were tapering off, and by ten, everything had been cleaned up. I helped put away tables and chairs as my mom cleared food away. Shortly after, the television accompanied my parents and me as we watched the nightly news. The time had come, I just didn't know how to bring it up.

"So will you be staying tonight?" my mom asked.

"Sorry, no. Mitch and Nadia will be back soon, and then we'll head back."

My mother smiled in a cute, impressive smile. "I sure like that girl, Oliver. What an impression she left with Nana, eating her pudding and all. I hope she stays around."

"Mom," I hurried before she continued, "I need to speak to you and Dad about something."

My mother started beaming. My father barely moved from the TV. After a gentle nudge from my mother, he finally turned the set off.

And there they were, right before me. I gulped hard before I spoke.

"Something happened to me in New York," I started. My mother's beam started to fade into concern. "Something I couldn't imagine would happen to me." I was struggling.

My mother reached over and patted my knee. "Are you alright?"

"That's not really what's important right now," I tried to continue. "There is something I am fighting about myself and it's hard to think of the words."

My father's face turned at the words I spoke; his eyes sunk down into my eyes and burrowed deep into my chest. "You can tell us, son," he asked, but I think he suspected something.

I gulped. "This is so much harder than I thought."

When I said it out loud, both of the expressions on my parents' faces dropped to thick, wordless silence.

"I was attacked about a month ago."

"What kind of attack?" my mother asked, but I cut her off.

"Please, I love you both, but I need to say this and then you can ask questions after." I didn't like being so stern, but my courage was there, and I needed to let it out. "I was attacked while I ran in Central Park one morning. I wasn't hurt so bad, but the experience changed me."

"Changed?" my mother squeaked out. "And why on earth were you running? Did you have your inhaler?"

"Yes. But don't worry about that."

My father looked at my mother and they exchanged looks. "Well, I expected something like this. You live in New York."

I was a little confused.

"But when he brought home that lovely girl, I really thought. . ." My mom stifled a choke in her throat.

My father reached over and put his arm around her and lovingly stroked her shoulder. "Oliver, it must take a lot of courage to come to us like this. And as your parents, we will always be there for you, however you choose to live."

"I'm not following you," I answered. It was like they had already had this discussion without me.

My father furrowed his brow and looked at me. "We always knew you were different, Oliver. And I bit my lip when you said you wanted to go to New York and be a philosopher. And there is no excuse for my behavior toward it, and I worried that my son would be lost to me if we let you go. But it is your life and not ours. So, if you need to live a lifestyle that will make you happy, we support it."

"You think I want to live like this?"

"We know that some things you can't choose," my mother came in.

"Wait, what are you talking about? I didn't choose this, and I would never choose this. It's the hardest thing I've ever had to face."

"Oh, my sweet boy," my mother said toward me.

"Mom?" I was confused again. "I don't think you understand what happened to me. Seems that the only one that really understands is Nadia."

My mother now looked very confused. "Nadia? She's this way, too?"

"Well, yes, she helped discover it."

Both my parents had blank faces.

"Wait? Are we talking about the same thing?"

My parents sat in sympathy.

"I'm not gay." I felt stupid for catching on so late in the conversation. "Why does everyone think I'm gay?"

"It's okay, Oliver." My mother had calmed down considerably.

"No. Seriously." My hands were waving. "No, no, let me see if I can explain it. I have a condition, Mom."

"So, you're not…" My father had to reassure himself.

"Honest, Dad." I tried to calm him down. "But still, that doesn't matter. I know you would be accepting parents, like you always have been. I might need that same understanding when I tell you what is different about me."

My mother immediately put her hands up to her face, "Are you dying?"

"No, mom, geez, don't get all hysterical. Let me finish." I was thinking on my feet now. I didn't want her to freak out any more than she would. "I have a very rare condition. It's like diabetes, but different. I have a special diet."

"So, you are not a vegetarian anymore?" my father asked. "Thank God." The look of relief was evident.

"Dad, it is so much worse than that. What I have is about as opposite as you could be from being a vegetarian. I'm a… I'm a vampire."

Phew. The words came out. I did it. I couldn't believe it. There the words hung in the air like some strange cloud no one could see, a dissipating fart hovering uncom-fortably that everyone knew was there, but no one dared say anything.

I looked very intently at the expression on my parents' faces, but both looked like they were about to laugh. "Did you understand what I said?"

"Of course," my mother returned. "Oh, but honey, my heart was all fluttering to think you might be dying of something. You really gave me a good scare there for a moment."

"I'm serious."

My father messed up his hair and relaxed back in the recliner. "Son, thanks for the laugh. So much serious talk gets me all anxious."

I tried to clear my head. "It doesn't bother you if I drink people's blood."

"Well, let's really talk about this vampire thing, shall we?" My father turned and faced me. "Are we in danger right now?"

"No, Dad, I promise, I would never hurt you."

"Have you drunk people's blood?"

"Not really."

"Have you killed anyone?"

"No, of course not."

"Then I don't see a problem."

I looked from my father to my mother's face. She had a weak smile. I think she was concerned about my mental health. "What about you, Mom?" I asked.

"Oliver, I love you," she returned. "Just be careful and don't hurt anybody with this problem in your life."

"Really, that's all you have to say to me. Do you think I'm crazy?"

"Well, I can see that you are not. You are talking very rationally, but there have been many problems in your life that we have faced. If this is like any of the others, I think you will be fine."

"Mom, how can you say that?

My mother turned to me and patted my cheek. "Oliver, you are more than you think you are. I think if you manage this problem, any of the other problems you have ever encountered will be easy."

"But it's true, Mom," I said emphatically. I turned to my father. "You believe me, right?"

"I always have," he said as his hand steadied back on the remote.

I was in disbelief, but also in awe at my parents. They were so calm about everything. I loved them more tonight than I have ever in my life.

The back door squeaked open, and I saw Mitch enter with Nadia behind him on the phone.

"We've got to go," Mitch said with a strange hesitation.

"Yes, you're right." I turned to my parents and hugged them goodbye and promised to fill them in on details of my pending graduation as I got them.

As we headed back to the car, I saw Nadia's tense expression as she finished her conversation on the phone. She hung up and pulled my arm.

"He found her," she said.

"Who?" I asked stupidly.

"Jovanny found the girl that bit you."

20

ALLERGIC TO STRAWBERRI

"GIVE ME BEAUTY IN THE INWARD SOUL; MAY THE OUTWARD AND THE INWARD MAN BE AS ONE."

I felt anxious the entire way home. I was afraid of meeting this girl and doing something so terrible, so unthinkable, I was caught off guard when Mitch asked if I had talked to Sunnie.

"Huh?" I woke up out of my stewing coma. Sunnie? Oh yeah. I felt around for my phone, only remembering the last time I had it was when I jumped in the lake. I could only figure it was still in my soggy clothes piled on the bathroom floor, sizzling the circuitry inside. "Well, I'll work on one problem at a time, after we get to Jovanny's lair." I said this out loud just to make a mental memory, a commitment to talk with her later.

Manhattan looked so good, even though traffic was miserable, as always. It was nearing one in the morning when we crossed the George Washington Bridge and traveled to the

West Side of Central. I felt that time moved backward. I felt my anxiety fill my insides. Vampires should not have anxiety.

Mitch dropped us off close to where I figured Jovanny's bridge hid, close to Strawberry Fields. Nadia and I traveled quickly through the dark park. A storm moved over us, an eerie, ominous vibe to capture the moment. In novels, this night would make a perfect vampire encounter, creepy and windy. I even grew nervous.

Nadia followed closely the instructions Jovanny fed her through a text. After a blur of black-on-black images, I saw, clear as anything, my favorite path through the park. We were close and I took off. I began to run—it was the excitement of everything, the thrill of the hunt, possibly. But I wasn't thirsty for blood; I was anxious. I planned in my head vengeance and revenge and horrible cruelty, like an Underworld movie. It was unlike me to create so much anger, but I played up the vampire in me and kept it fueling.

But honestly, what was I going to do? That thought never crossed my mind. I wasn't vengeful. I wasn't blood-thirsty or cruel. Me, a failed philosophy major, what did I know about anger? I was searching to blame someone, but what would that change?

Nadia yelled behind me to slow down, but the bridge crept closer, and I stopped. A brief moment flashed—the night I caught sight of her there, the night I chased her away and found Jovanny. It was all so fresh in my mind.

Nadia tapped my shoulder. "Hey, jerk, I'm not as fast as you."

"Sorry," I replied without thinking, my mind still elsewhere.

"Oliver, can I say something?"

"Yeah. Go ahead."

My attention turned to where she stood. How different she looked under the smoky light, the little details stood out as she tightened her ponytail, wisps of black hair fell over her brow, her intense look created a tiny crease on her forehead.

She smiled uncomfortably and swept the long pieces from her face and placed them behind her ear. Her voice quieted down to a near whisper. Only the clicking of the katydids sounded around us. "Oliver, don't be an idiot."

"What?" I said confused.

"Promise me you will use your head. Think rationally about it."

"About what?"

Nadia made a sweet humph in her throat and walked forward. "I know what you want to do, but I don't want you to lose yourself in anger."

Anger? Was I really angry? Had she even seen me angry? Maybe she could see something else in my need to find this girl. "I think I can handle myself."

"I'm not worried about you," she clarified. "We don't know what happened to this girl. Take that into consideration."

"I'm confused. What do you think I would do?"

"Nothing exactly that I can think of," she explained. "But, Parker, you are about to confront the person who bit you. I can only think you are going to do something filled with revenge. Come on. That isn't you. This could change you. I don't want it to."

"Change me? How could this possibly change me from what I am now?"

"Whoa, Park." I could see the frustration on her face. "This is what I mean. I'm afraid it might. That's all. I like you how you are."

I looked directly in her eyes lit by the nightscape. "It's not because I kissed you?"

Nadia smirked. "What?"

"I know, I'm in the friend zone, but I kissed you, and I wanted to. It was an impulse, I admit it, but it felt right, even if I was weird about it."

"Wait a minute," she came back at me. "Have you been thinking about that the whole time? Not about ripping this girl apart?"

"Why would I do that—" I tried to answer, but she pressed her lips tight on mine preventing my speech. I guess that was one way to shut me up. The surprise disappeared to impulse to wandering until I didn't care and went with it.

When she pulled away, I looked at her dark silhouette, more confused than ever. She turned and walked away without a word.

I stood in shock and nearly forgot why we had come to the bridge in the first place. I walked dumbly after her, and before I knew it, we were standing at the hidden door in silence. I kept staring at her.

"Hey," Jovanny opened the door and woke me back to reality. "Hurry, come in." He ushered us into the small lit room. Inside the small brick room, filled with eclectic odds and ends, there sat a girl, the girl that bit me.

Everything in the room disappeared away from sight. Everything from the last few minutes faded. All my focus, all my energy was held onto this small girl.

She sat on a broken stool looking at me. Her hollow black eyes filled with hate and pain and anger. I could see the pale-ish skin, now marked with scrapes and scratches, sunk deep in her face. Her clothes were the same black tattered strips from the first time I saw her. And there was an unmistakable smell around her—an odor worse than expected, the smell of rotting meat.

"You look better," she remarked in a rather bitter voice. "Do you taste any better?"

I felt the insult but didn't know how to respond.

"How long have you had her?" Nadia asked Jovanny.

Jovanny went and sat on the crammed plaid couch at the end of the room. "Couple hours. A few of us were outperforming near the Pond when I spotted her. She was pretty wily, but with all of us, she didn't have a chance."

"I only stopped to watch the stupidity play out," the girl came back at him.

Jovanny smiled smugly. "Whatever worked."

I now could see her hands tied up in interweaving knots.

"Do you have to tie her?" I don't know where the compassion came from. Shouldn't I hate this girl?

"Oh yes. She's like a crazed animal if I don't have her tied."

I didn't like seeing anyone tied. She was a tiny teenager. Was it necessary?

The girl's eyes intensified as if she could sense my motives or read my thoughts. I wasn't sure what to think of her.

"Can I ask your name?"

"Her name is Strawberri Jones," Jovanny stated. "She didn't tell me anything when I first asked, but I found her ID hanging around her pocket. I did a quick search on the internet, and it showed a missing poster with her picture posted from some family blog. Turns out she's sixteen, from Brooklyn, and a hell of a singer."

Strawberri looked surprised at all this knowledge.

"Is this true?" I asked.

The girl just sized me up again and said nothing, but by the reaction I knew enough.

"How long have you been missing?"

"Four months," Jovanny stated again looking at the blog.

"Only four? And do you know what happened to you?" This time the girl's head went down to her chest. I caught a very faint "No."

"Do you even know what you are?"

She looked up again and met me square in the eyes. "I'm a monster, that's what. And I don't know what you want with me, but if you are trying to kill me, forget it. I've tried and I still can't die, so why don't you all just leave me alone!"

It was Nadia that came to her side. She quickly took hold of Strawberri's hands and held them. The girl didn't object. "Listen to me," she started all serious. "Come on. You're not a monster; you're special, unique, and beautiful. You just don't know it yet. Do you look at me as a monster?"

"You're not like me."

"I'm just like you, promise. And there is nothing wrong with acting out on your natural instincts for blood."

Strawberri looked forlorn. "But I've killed people."

"So what?" Nadia came back. "That is what you're supposed to do. It's okay. You shouldn't feel guilty about it. There are things in this world worse than death."

Strawberri just looked at her, trying to understand.

A had an idea. "When you woke up, where were you?"

"I was in this park," she returned to me. "I haven't left it. I have been too scared."

"So, you didn't know how to live or what happened to you."

She shook her head. "All I know is I was starving, and I needed food, but I couldn't eat. I started to suck on birds and squirrels I would kill. But then the thirst came, and I tried to suck on people."

"Is that when you came after me?" I asked.

"Yes, but you were the worst thing I had ever tasted, worse than Brussels sprouts. I'm so sorry I attacked you, but I couldn't help my thirst. After that I thought everyone might taste like you, so then I tried to kill myself, but nothing worked. I hate myself!" She went into a fit and tried to claw herself. Nadia again grabbed her.

"Jovanny?" Nadia asked. "Can you get in touch with Krysztof? I think she needs to meet with him."

Jovanny sat straight up at the request, and soon he was on the phone with him.

Nadia came back to me and whispered. "Is this what you expected?"

I didn't have a response at first. "She's just like me," I returned.

"She has no idea what to do with this life. I have to try to make it better. Is that okay with you?"

She was sincere, but why was she asking me? I could see the wretchedness of the situation and deteriorated state she had spun into. And unlike me, there was no hope for her. She was a full vampire without a chance to get away from it.

I couldn't believe my feelings. I wasn't sure want would happen when I met her, but I didn't expect this. Where was my satisfaction with blame? I couldn't blame her.

"Please help her," I replied. And my anger went away for good.

21

A SUNNIE MORNING

"THE HOTTEST LOVE HAS THE COLDEST END."

Strawberri was something else. I wasn't prepared for everything she had to say. She was mad at the world, much like I was, but her anger was unbridled and her temper flaring. The things she'd been through and the suicides she attempted were rather graphic. I'd never heard anything so awful, not even on HBO.

Nadia, Jovanny, and I talked with her deep in the night about her problems. Nadia tried where she could to clear up misconceptions. Krysztof and his crew came and collected her around four in the morning and took her back to wherever he took people like that.

As Strawberri and Krysztof were leaving, I silently observed Jovanny and Nadia talking pretty seriously. I felt in the way. Jovanny and Nadia were dating. Or were they? I didn't really know. I'd rather stay out of weird situations like that. Then it hit me, I might be the cause of the conversation.

I suddenly felt very uneasy and ditched out of there without a second thought.

The walk felt awesome. I loved New York at night; the city didn't love everyone, but it loved me. It was a hard-earned love, granted. The noise of the city and the lights, the honk every twenty seconds, the smell of the subway that permeated everything until you couldn't smell it anymore, the pedestrian-ruled crosswalks and the smothering garbage heaped on the street waiting to be picked up. But beyond that I witnessed the little things that made it special, flowers growing through cracks in the sidewalk, the stonework that has witnessed eras pass and become storytellers of history. This city wasn't for everyone, but it was for me.

I took a deep breath and looked around me. Everything was still alive at night. I picked up my feet and started to run, testing my endurance. I didn't head to my apartment either, though I should have.

I ran directly to Sunnie's. My guilt caught up to me in the park and through the streets. I needed to talk to her and explain to her everything that happened. This was going to suck, I kept thinking, but I couldn't deal with my reality if I didn't face it.

It was about half past five in the morning when I reached her steps. My strength was gone. It had been a long day, and I needed sleep like everyone else. I was also very afraid of the sun coming and scorching me like a tamale.

I went for her buzzer and stopped. What a stupid thing I was about to do? Who rings at five in the morning? But I was running out of time. The sun had nowhere to go when it surfaced the ocean, and so I buzzed her, breaking the harmony of the waking birds.

I waited.

There was nothing.

I buzzed again—longer than before. I must be the most irritating person in the whole—

"Hello?" came a crackly voice.

"Sunnie?"

"Sunnie?" she said. "Just a sec."

Now I felt like a real shmuck waking up her roommate. It took a while for anyone to come to the intercom.

"Hello?" Sunnie's sweet voice came through loud and clear.

"Sunnie? It's Oliver."

Immediately the com went dead. She had hung up on me. She must hate me. I had screwed up the relationship before it really ever started. At least that was a consolation, that I never got so invested before she broke my heart.

I began to walk away when the door opened behind me. I turned just in time for the impact. Sunnie wrapped her arms tightly around me.

"Ollie. I was so worried."

"What do you mean?"

Sunnie let go. Her messy morning hair stuck up around her tight bun, and I couldn't mistake the dark circles around her eyes. I didn't want to imagine what I just put this girl through.

"I tried to call you yesterday, but your phone just went to voicemail. I'm so sorry that I wasn't here."

"Oh, sorry?" I was rather confused.

"I stayed at Elsie's Friday night. We talked and introduced me to your world and everything, and we stayed up really late. I met her sister, who is absolutely the best, and I think you would appreciate her. Did you know she is going to Julliard? People like that make me crazy you know, smart and insanely talented."

I let her ramble around as I pondered what she had said. Through the mindless sputtering it occurred to me, she wasn't even here. She doesn't know I ditched her. I could walk away from this without a scratch.

"…I woke up around eleven and I felt so bad, believe me when I say I'm so sorry. And I was clear across town, and I figured you would understand, but I never dreamed I wouldn't talk to you. Then I started thinking that your kind wouldn't like you dating me and then I thought about that Nadia and how much she doesn't like me. And holy, there would be a big vampire fight, and I tried so many times to call and say I'm so sorry—"

I hushed her up with my finger on her lips. "Don't worry. I'm fine."

"Where's your phone?"

"It got fried when I jumped in a lake."

"Did you try to cross it?"

"Huh?"

"Vampires aren't allowed to cross water."

"Really…" I hadn't heard that one. I might check that out in the *Fact or Fiction* pamphlet.

"Will you forgive me?" Sunnie looked as if she was about to cry. She pretended to be such a tough girl, but she was a marshmallow.

But here, this weird problem swallowed me again. I really didn't know what to do. My brain was mixed up between two realities: Sunnie's and Nadia's. When have I ever been between two girls? With Nadia I had real possibilities that I'd never considered, and with Sunnie I was back to my comfortable self. Stuck in the middle without the charisma to choose.

"Of course I'll forgive you," I said taking her back in my arms and holding her. I swore several times in my head, but as I figured it, my situation was no different than it had been the previous day. As long as I didn't tell either girl about anything, it would be fine. Just like a situational comedy. Of course, this would eventually blow up and I might need to come clean, but there was a slim possibility nothing might happen. It wasn't in me to willingly deceive people, but I also didn't like to create drama. It was still possible everything would blow over and return to normal. It could theoretically happen. Theoretically.

At least I had time to think about it. All I needed was time. Time would save me.

My face began to sting and then my arm. The sunlight streaks of morning hit me, and I yelled in pain.

"What's wrong?" Sunnie backed away.

"I can't be in the sun," I returned heading for the shadows on the building.

"I'm sorry, I completely forgot," Sunnie returned hurrying me away. "Come inside."

"I wouldn't want to intrude."

"Don't worry. My roommate sleeps until noon on Sundays."

I walked up to her apartment. This time I was the one she helped in. Even the few streams of sunlight left my arm sizzling. I could see tiny little blisters forming right above my elbow. This burn hurt worse than the others, and I couldn't figure why. I didn't think it had anything to do with the proximity of the sun, but that was all I had to blame.

She laid me on her sofa and placed a blanket on me. I must have looked tired because she left me alone. I don't remember falling asleep, but I woke to a cool sensation on my arm, maybe a cold compress placed on my burn.

Sunnie sat on the floor next to me with a small bowl of ice water rinsing out the cloth and placing it back on my arm.

"Thank you," I remarked. "That's really sweet of you. I don't think it really works, but it's a nice idea."

She turned a little pink in the cheeks and went back tending to my burn. "I got a few phone calls for you."

"For me?" I returned nervously. "Who could be calling you to get to me?"

"One was your friend Mitch, who got my number from your phone to tell you that your phone is working, and another call was from your father telling me that he contacted Mitch to get my number so he could call to tell me to tell you that your phone is working, and he has it and will bring it on Friday."

"That was nice of him to call. What time is it?"

"About five. I didn't know you would sleep that long."

"Oh, sorry," I tried to sit up. "It was a long night, and I have a very screwy sleep schedule."

"I understand," she returned. "Well, I'm trying to understand. Would you like anything to drink?"

I looked at her with a strange expression.

"Oh sorry," she returned. "Not really what I meant, but is there anything I can get for you?"

"I don't think you will have anything that will satisfy," I said.

"Probably true. I don't eat very much meat, but my roommate is a total carnivore. She might have something."

"I can feel my hunger, but it's not as bad as it has been."

"How was your night?" Sunnie asked as she entered the kitchen to rummage through the fridge. "I never got a chance to ask."

"Oh, it was interesting," I chose through my words carefully. "I met the girl that bit me."

"What?" Sunnie said as she ran back to me. "That is incredible. What did you do?"

"Nothing," I replied. "I couldn't do anything. She was so pathetic I couldn't do anything. I pity her."

"Whoa, I thought you might kill her," she said. "Shred her up or something."

"Well, that's gruesome," I returned. The idea was really horrifying to me. "Really? Do you think I could do that? I wish you had a better idea of real vampirism."

I think she felt a sting from my comment, though I meant nothing by it. "Well, Elsie took me to The Cell on Friday."

"She did what? You went there? Do you know what kind of place that is?"

"Well, I had always thought the reputation was a myth, but it turned out more terrifying than I could realize."

"What happened?" I don't remember how I appeared standing above her.

"Nothing really. I got really drunk, I think. My little frame can't take much alcohol. I don't remember much of the night and woke up with a banging headache. That's one of the reasons I didn't come to your family thing."

I quickly grabbed her arm and examined it. In the top crease above her elbow, sure as ever, a small red dot big enough for a needle. "They drained you."

"What do you mean?" Her voice shrunk a little.

"The really intoxicated ones get drained of blood. That is what the vampires drink there."

Sunnie looked at me and a queer look came across her face. "Are you telling me that you could taste my blood without biting me?"

"Well, I guess," I stopped. "But that's not the point."

"Ollie, then you wouldn't hurt me. It is a simple solution."

"You might think that, but I might throw-up at the image of it being your blood." I sat down again with my head in my hands. "Don't worry about it. I should probably get home anyway."

"I understand," Sunnie said in a calm voice, compared to my outburst. "A few more things, you got another phone call from a guy named Jovanny,"

My stomach plummeted. "What did he say?"

"Just told me that you need to call him. Do you want to use my phone?"

I stood up and checked out the window. There looked to be enough shadows to cover me to the subway station. "Ah sure," I returned unthinking. She handed me her phone, which had a skin of blue plaid with skulls and kitties on it. How appropriate. I looked through the last phone calls received, saw all the numbers, purposing skipping Jovanny's number and hitting Mitch's.

Mitch answered.

"Hey Jovanny. What's up?" I said loudly, maybe over-dramatically.

"Ollie, you piece of shit. You know it's me, don't you," Mitch returned.

"Yes, this is just Sunnie's phone until I get mine back."

"You are such a jerk! Are you too chicken to talk to that man after all he did for you? He found the girl that bit you and then of course you kissed his girl!"

"Does he know that?" I said back, ignoring the looks from Sunnie.

"Oh yes, quite the repayment. He came to your apartment looking for you."

"But you led me to think that she—" I stopped short.

"I just told you which I preferred. You're a—" and then he let it roll. The noises and expletives that filled the other side of the phone were embarrassing. He was doing it on purpose to catch me at something.

"Thanks, I'll follow up tomorrow. Bye." And hung up mid-swear.

"Are you okay?"

I huffed. "No. I need to meet with somebody." I turned toward the door. "Thanks for everything."

I looked toward Sunnie, who looked so lost in words. "Can I say one more thing?" I nodded. "Your father called me Nadia."

I didn't know how to respond. My stomach hit the bottom.

She smiled meekly. "We'll talk about it later, when you have sorted through everything, okay?"

I returned the smile, and she closed the door in my face.

$$22$$

A PIED PIPER

"HOW MANY ARE THE THINGS I CAN DO WITHOUT!"

After I returned to my apartment, I checked my email. Dean Fessinger wrote me a scathing reply to my test results and a deep reprimand about the importance of my involvement in the council meeting on Wednesday.

And down spiraled the last of my will. It was time for me to give up. So, I sat back down on the couch and stayed there for two days.

I didn't have a phone to bother me; no one could get a hold of me or chew me out for whatever I might or might not have done, and I couldn't think where Mitch was—figured he would be at my place like always. Although, he left his games, and that was a blessing. I played until I was dizzy and then slept on and off. I thawed out a big rump roast I had in the freezer and slowly sucked on the juices until it was no longer red. I didn't care about work anymore. I should have, but didn't, and school was over for me. My stomach turned at the thought of a council meeting I needed to attend but wasn't going to. As I figured, my academic career was finished, and I'd pack up all my crap and move back down to Lake Hopatcong, live with my parents, and work at the small shake shop like I did in high school.

Tuesday afternoon I woke up to pounding on the door. I stuck one of the couch cushions over my head and pretended not to hear. After a few minutes I heard muffled talking outside, and then the lock began to turn.

"Park?" a voice came rushing in, a pleasant voice I was afraid of hearing—Nadia's. "Oliver?" I heard her stop before my couch. I felt her eyes on me, penetrating through my coverage until she could see my failures. "I found him. He's here."

"He ain't dead, is he?" a different voice said. I took off the pillow just to see my superintendent, Steve Kabrinski, or Super Steve as I called him, looking down on me. "Guess not."

"Thank you for your help," Nadia dispensed him away and closed the door. She came back to the couch and sat sideways next to my feet. "Are you okay?" she asked, gently tapping at my toe.

I placed the pillow back over my head and rolled over.

"Park, you need to drink something."

I ignored her.

"Why don't you tell me what happened."

"No," I muttered in the pillow. A few seconds later, I felt my body being tugged away from the couch and I landed in a heap on the floor. "Stop it!"

"You stop it, you big jerk," she yelled and slugged me in the arm.

"You didn't need to do that."

"Yes, I did," she justified. "Parker, what the sh——?"

"Stop calling me Parker!" I snapped. "I'm not some superhero—I am a pathetic version of myself."

"Get up. You need to shower. You are starting to smell. This body is not as forgiving as a living body."

"I don't care."

"Your muscles deteriorate if you don't feed yourself, and your skin is dead, and the stink is crazy."

"Why are you here anyway?" I threw the pillow at her.

She dodged easily. "Good question. I didn't come here to argue with you, but you are being such an ass stewing here in your thoughts. Get up! You didn't go to work either."

"I thought I might see someone there."

She threw the pillow back and hit me square in the chin. "You coward. Was this how you were before I got to know you?"

"Maybe?" I answered.

She left to my kitchen. My cupboards open, my fridge, and the blender. She was making me something to drink. I just sank my head back on the floor and closed my eyes.

"Here," I opened my eyes to blood red liquid. The smell overpowered my senses. I had really starved myself the last few days. I couldn't think of when the last time I really ate anything was. The taste was deep and filling, and within a minute it was gone.

"Thank you," I muttered.

"Does that help your mood?"

"It might," I returned with a smile.

"If you want men to be happy, just make sure they're fed. That rule is true in any situation."

A small laugh jumped from my mouth. It surprised me.

"Seriously, Parker, what happened to you? You just fell apart."

My smile faded and I swallowed hard. "I'm a mess." I laid my head back on the floor, sinking again into the despair of my reality. "I'm lost. I miss my Lexapro, followed with a Clonazepam, and chased down with Mountain Dew. Sunnie knows I kissed you and knows I lied about it, my parents don't care, they just think I'm a hypochondriac. True, I might have cried wolf a few times, but it bothers me that they don't care when I'm serious. And I'm not going to graduate, Nadia." I finally admitted to myself. The rush of reality hit my head and made me dizzy.

"Graduating?" Nadia's voice was soft as she contemplated what I said. "You're worried about that? That's easy. I can help with that. A few phone calls and it will be back on. Even if you miss a few classes, there is always next semester. Just extend it a little—"

"I just want to hide in a hole," I admitted. "I'll need a new job and new professors, a new major. But I shouldn't care anymore. And I don't know what to say to Sunnie."

"I can't help you with that."

"Tell me about your human relationship," I blurted out. "The one that turned out so badly."

She blushed. I didn't think vampires could do that. "No, I don't think so," she stood up and went back to the couch.

"I think it would make me feel better if I knew."

"Oliver, can I be frank?" she asked. I nodded. "Sunnie is comfortable for you in your old life, but you need to step forward. She's not my taste. I don't hate her, really, she's okay, but she wants a fantasy. That really bothers me. The person she sees in you is not real, so how do you think you could have an honest relationship if she doesn't know the real you."

"How do you know this?" She was dodging my question, and I wanted an honest answer.

"It's more complicated than that," she admitted. "It's ongoing."

"Ongoing?"

She rolled her eyes in the back of her head. I could see the grief she wore because of the situation.

"Please, I need to know."

"Will you promise you won't tell?"

Tell? Who was she thinking I would tell? I didn't know anyone. "Yes," I answered.

She sighed, thinking. "When I was brought to New York after my bite, I hung around some dark people. There are some great underground clubs you can find in New York, and I had no fear of anything, because what else could happen to me? Which is completely true, may I add?" She tied up her black, sleek hair with a pencil as she talked. "I met someone there who I found funny and unusual, and I like that, a genuine character unlike anyone else. He was a vampire, with the things he talked about, but it was obvious after a while that I had been interpreting him completely wrong. He was not specifically talking about himself, but about a character he was portraying in a game."

"A game? Like a video game?"

She tilted her head hoping I had caught on. "No, in a real action adventure he had created."

And suddenly I knew where this was heading.

"I was curious and got to know him better. But he found out my secret by simple deduction. He is such a deep thinker and figured it out. He romanced me for a while, but it got too smothering. I turned to leave, but he approached me and actually asked me to bite him. I didn't think I was allowed to do that. I considered his situation with no real family around. If anything, I could have a friend around to help with my loneliness. So, I did it."

"You're talking about Jovanny, aren't you?" I slid out the connection.

"Yes," she admitted. Her hands went through the few random hair strands slipping from her bun. "And it is just getting worse. I can't get away from it. I have overwhelming guilt. He didn't tell me about his daughter."

"He has a kid?"

"Yeah. She's about six now. I hate that I bit him. I hate that he turned, though Vampirism suits him well. I've never seen one so good at misleading and hunting, like the pied piper, if I could make any analogy to anyone. I feel disgusted and used, and I'm still mad he didn't tell me about his daughter. To think of that little girl growing up to find out what her dad is now is horrifying."

And I slowly watched the bricks that held up her life crumble before me. Nadia folded down around her knees, her head pressed against them. She completely fell apart in front of me. It was hard to watch. She couldn't crumble; she was my Rock of Gibraltar. I was the vulnerable one, right? What could I do?

I got up off the ground and sat next to her on the couch. It wasn't my intent, being unfamiliar with feminine emotions, but I didn't like witnessing the collapse of such a solid individual. I stretched out my arm and wrapped her tight. I didn't know vampires could cry, but I was wrong about that too. Aside from everything in my life right now, this was the right thing to do, and it felt good doing the right thing for a change. The goodness was still there. I wasn't damned yet.

At that moment I was the strong one. She now depended on me to hold up the bridge of strength. It was a place I always wanted to be, but never felt adequate. If I had a vision of my life before now, I would act as the strong figure of the family, like my father—always the example of strength, possibly living in a small town like Hopatcong, not New York. Was I really that different from my father? I always thought I was, but in my core, I wanted what he wanted.

With Nadia wrapped in my arms, I let the emotions sink in. Feeling her tears release next to me reminded me of our fragile human nature. Emotions and situations were still present in our state, but the reality of the ugly nature of what we have become only cemented the fact that I needed her more than ever.

"I don't know what to do?" she whispered in my shirt.

"Neither do I," I returned. "I guess we'll figure it out."

She pulled away. I looked at her and loved those dark, smiling eyes. I wanted so badly to kiss her, but played it smart this time and resisted the all-natural urge that pulled me to her at such a fragile moment.

"We have one more treatment tomorrow at nine," she said to me.

I almost forgot what she was talking about. "Oh, right. Got it."

"Now, will you please go take a shower and eat something proper?"

I smiled. "Sorry, yes."

"And go to work."

"Yikes. Really?" I asked.

"You need to for your own conscience."

"Wow, you do know me."

"We are not that different, you and I," she said as she stood up to leave. "As much as you like to think." She reached the door before she solemnly said, "Thank you, Oliver. I won't call you Parker if you don't like it. But I still think it is fitting, since you got me to talk about something I swore never to say."

I met her at the door. "You can call me Parker. I don't mind if it comes from you."

She smiled. There was a brief pause where I did nothing else but stare at her. And she stared at me back. But then she turned and walked away down the stairwell.

23

THE FESS MESS

"NO MAN UNDERTAKES A TRADE HE HAS NOT
LEARNED, EVEN THE MEANEST; YET EVERYONE
THINKS HIMSELF SUFFICIENTLY QUALIFIED FOR
THE HARDEST OF ALL TRADES, THAT OF
GOVERNMENT."

I took Nadia's advice and took a shower. I creamed myself
with whatever product I had and actually cared what I did with
my hair; it took a few seconds more than my messy fingered-
through look, but I was okay with it.

When the sun went down, I went shopping for food,
special food from a few of the markets suggested in the cards
and pamphlets I received from the first day. The selection was
amazing. I bought way more than I should, but my appetite
was adventurous and sought things I would never try in any
normal circumstances—Xidato, Aegean Aima root, and
something called Migliaccio—a sweet pig blood pancake.
Whatever Nadia made just whet my appetite for some sweet
and juicy, iron-filled blood, pass out or not.

I considered contacting Sunnie, I even passed her apartment but continued to walk by. I figured I needed a good satisfying meal before I approached that bridge. I honestly didn't know what I was going to do. I certainly had a lot to think about, and some satisfying food and a good relaxing book should help, like George Orwell or Stephen King.

But, yet again, my brain wouldn't stop thinking. My mind wouldn't shut off. Everything hinged on Wednesday. I couldn't get away from work again, and I had to talk with Sunnie, or at least see her. I couldn't get over the serious anxiety about my meeting with Dean Fessinger, Professor Martin, and the whole tribal council; and then my exchange— THE blood exchange that could change everything. I needed discipline. The lifestyle was something to get used to, just like when I became a vegetarian, which devastated my mother and her homemade meatloaf. But if this worked, if there was a chance for me to become human again, to taste sweet Oreos again, I promised myself I would taste Mom's meatloaf and be more forgiving to her for eating it.

Discipline. Focus. Discipline and focus.

And then I hated myself, dwelling on how much my life sucked and how many problems I had caused, how many people it affected. I began to make a list in my head.

Nadia hated me for dating Sunnie.

Sunnie hated me for lying to her.

Jovanny hated me for kissing Nadia.

Sunnie would hate me if she knew I had kissed Nadia. *But, come on, we weren't exclusive. We weren't even serious.*

My parents will hate me when they find out I'm not graduating. *But I could graduate eventually… probably.*

My boss Warren has always hated me.

And Mitch might not hate me, but he won't be happy that I passed his game using his ultra-powerful guy he created with a cheat code.

The worst thing, I didn't know what I could do about any of it.

I fell asleep with the book on my face.

Wednesday morning, luck was not with me. I prayed for rain, but there was not a cloud in the sky. This would make things difficult, since I needed to be at the council meeting by eleven. I had an umbrella, my solar screening Hot Topic bomber jacket, and I had lathered myself with some SPF-Vampire sunscreen that I didn't think worked. With the sun so bright as it was with no shade in sight, it would be tricky, and I would need to be careful.

I would have to thank Nadia and her designer sense for the clothes I wore: a sharp blue dress shirt with a blended tie and smooth twill flat front trousers. I never owned anything nice like this. I used the Philosophy major for a lot of my fashion excuses. But I had to say, I think I looked really good—a handsome version of myself that I never let out. I looked like a competent, smart individual, when really, I was a complete mess.

I couldn't have been more careful outside on the street in the shadows or under the awnings at the window shops. Before I believed it, I was in the West building outside of Professor Martin's office waiting for my fate.

"Hey, Brixby," I was hailed down the hall by a man in a scrubby Black Keys tee shirt. It was David Littlelight, the marijuana plantation dreamer. "Man, haven't seen you since you took off that night."

"Yeah," I quickly commented. "Things got pretty intense there for a minute. I hope everything went well."

"Be glad you left. Sarah and Rachel just started arguing, and then we ditched studying altogether. I can't really remember what we did—the night from then on was kind of sketchy—" which meant to me that he got drunk and passed out on some random couch. "But what's with the tie?"

"Just meeting with a few people—"

"Hey, did you read about Fess?" he interrupted.

"Fess?" meaning Fessinger, we all knew the slang. "Why? What do you know?" I wasn't meaning to get defensive, but does he know about the email he sent me? About my meeting to determine if I'm graduating or not?

"He's totally missing."

"What?"

"Hey, I read it this morning. Hunter sent out a wide email to everyone. I guess he's been gone for a few days. His wife doesn't know where he is."

"What?" I repeated, more to myself.

"Here," he reached into his pocket and brought out his phone. He started searching through his apps on the touch screen and brought up the email titled from the Office of the President of Hunter College—Julita Bliss-Vega.

> *Dear Beloved Students,*
>
> *As many of you have heard, a tragic disappearance of one of our beloved professors, Harold B. Fessinger, Chair of the College of Philosophy, disappeared from his residence late Sunday afternoon. Please keep him and his family in your thoughts and prayers at this very tender time. We hope for the best outcome in this situation.*

As for staffing during this time, Professor Shami Tahassapour will act as chair in his stead until the outcome of this terrible situation can find resolution.

Please be very delicate to those in grief, the college specifically and any close to those who have known him.

If you have seen or might know or know of someone who might have any information, please contact the NYPD Police department, Campus Police, or myself for further investigation—

"I can't believe it," I muttered. I was almost knocked off my feet.

"You okay?" David asked, seeing the state of me.

"That is who I'm supposed to meet with." I went right to his office and knocked. There was no answer of course, but I felt weird not doing it. I slowly opened the door. "Fess?"

Dean Fessinger's office was a heaping mess, but that was how it always had been—piles of papers stacked on the corner of his desk, stacks of books with tabs where he needed to mark it or had found something of importance. I remembered very well in my junior year taking one of his classes on Philosophy and Psychology and pulling book after book with these marked passages. The man had yet to discover Power Point. I looked briefly around.

"What are you doing?" David asked at the door.

"I don't know," I stated the truth. "I thought it might help…" I paused midsentence. Down on a few yellow post-it notes, I noticed my name with a date and time. The date was Sunday. I never met him on Sunday. Oh, no. Oh wait! A silent scream echoed in my head. Why was this here? When had I decided to meet up with him on Sunday? I don't even have a phone with me.

Sunday was the day I received that email, but I remembered it had been sent Friday afternoon; I just didn't receive it until then. So how did he…?

And then it hit me. And a wave of very deep trouble barreled down on me. I slid the post-it from the table without detection and left the office. Was I being set up? But Fessinger wasn't murdered, just missing. But if they go through his email, they might see what he wrote, they might think I want retaliation, and they might find out the truth about me, the monster I really am. But I've never harmed anyone. I've never bitten or sucked any living human. What was this all about? The test? About graduation? Who cares about that anymore?

"Hey, David," I called out as I left the office. "Can I borrow your phone?"

He eyed me before handing it over. "Yeah, so what's going on?" he asked rather cold.

"I wish I knew," I returned. "Honest. I don't have anything to do with his disappearance, but I might know someone who does."

David's face went white. "Really?"

"I don't know," I said dialing. My stupid stubby fingers always picked up a few extra numbers, so it took a few times.

It rang and then went to voicemail. It's because I was calling from a weird number. I hung up and called again. This time Mitch answered.

"Yes…" it was dry and tired.

"Mitch. It's Oliver."

"Ollie. Where are you calling me from—"

"Sorry, don't have time to explain. I need a favor. I don't have Nadia's number. Can you call her and have her meet me at the Wexler in fifteen minutes?"

"I'll try," he scratched out.

I hung up and handed it back to David. "Thanks."

He looked rather nervous, but said, "If there's anything I can help with."

That was the first time a straight sentence came out of his mouth. "Sure," I said and patted him on the shoulder.

I turned and headed directly over the bridge toward the Wexler Library.

"Oliver?" Beth came from around the front desk and gave me an unexpected hug. "Where have you been? We tried to call you, but it went straight to voicemail."

"Sorry, I lost my phone," I returned, shirking off the hug.

"I thought, well, I thought you might have gone missing like that professor."

"Nope, still here. Where's Warren?" I asked quickly.

Beth turned around to Deborah, the cat lady. "You haven't seen Warren, have you?"

"Sorry," she replied. "Must be his day off."

"But he hasn't been here all week," Beth returned.

My stomach knotted again. "Great," I muttered. "They might be targeting them."

"What was that?" Beth asked.

"Nothing. Sorry. Thinking out loud again."

"Oliver, what is going on?" she demanded.

My mind scrambled with the details. I almost forgot she had asked me a question. "Listen, I need your help. Is there a conference room open?"

"Seventh floor isn't being used."

"Perfect. I'm meeting someone here. Her name is Nadia. When she gets here, will you direct her there for me?"

"Sure," she returned concerned, but I didn't have time to care about it. I smiled before I turned toward the elevators.

On the seventh floor was the art section and galleries. Here, so near the end of school, it sat practically barren. Only a few wandering souls were lurking about. I found a spare computer and logged in. Sure enough, I had a ton of emails to weed through. Most were junk, and a few held my interest, but I could get back to them later. It looked like the same old stuff. So, I went over to a web browser and logged on to Facebook. I usually never touched Facebook; I only remember starting up an account when an old girlfriend of mine told me she put pictures of us on the site. I wasn't too thrilled about it and checked it out. I did remember I could instant message Mitch and it would go directly to his phone.

... pop...
"Hey Buddy." He wrote.

"Did you get a hold of Nadia?" Enter... and I waited.

... pop...
"She's across town but is coming. Are you in trouble?"

I paused. "We'll see. Where have you been? I haven't seen you."

... pop...
"Busy. Have you seen Sunnie?"

"No," I typed back, but it was just a matter of time.

... pop...

"Laters."

He dropped out of the conversation. Mitch has never been really busy in his life, so it confused me for a moment of what could be taking up his time.

I browsed around Facebook for a minute or two trying to eat away the time. I discovered the horrifying reality that there were a lot more photos of me posted than I liked. I waded through the friend requests and ignored most all of them. Why would these people that I might have known for two seconds in Elementary school care what I am doing now? I got aggravated and logged off.

I paced around like an impatient lion, stepped in the conference room, looked out the windows, and stewed in my thoughts. The more I pondered, the darker the feelings became.

"Oliver?" Beth's voice woke me from my agitation. I turned and watched Beth lead Nadia in and close the door behind her.

Nadia looked terribly concerned as she set down her shopping bags and purse on the long conference table. "Are you okay, Parker?"

I was gripping the chair in front of me so hard the leather had indents from my nails.

"Parker, what's going—"

"Please don't call me Parker," I said as I tried to stay calm. "Not right now."

"Fine," she returned a little hurt.

"What did you tell them?"

She moved her hands to her hips. "What are you talking about?"

"What did you tell them about my situation?"

"Tell who and what?" she snapped back. She could fight just as well as I could. I think she would beat me actually. "Honestly, Park—Oliver, I have no idea what you're talking about."

I was nervous, but she had to know. "You told me. You told me when I saw you that you would take care of the problem of me graduating."

"No," she corrected. "I said I could help."

"How?"

"Well, I was going to talk to Krysztof—"

"So, he knows?"

"Please let me finish," she yelled back.

"Fessinger's gone missing, and the police are going to think that I had something to do with it."

"Why?"

I pulled out the stcky note from my pocket and showed her. "I found this on his desk."

"You were in his office?"

"Well, yes, but that is beside the point. I only went in there to make sure he hadn't died or something in his office."

She looked over the note. "This is dated Sunday. I saw you last night."

"But who else knew?" I began pacing in my panic. "You are the only one I've confided in."

"There are others that know you're a vampire, not just me," she stood to face me. "What about Sunnie?"

"She wouldn't have the connections to pull off something like this, and you know that."

"Pull off what?" she chewed every word. "Sounds like you already concluded the guy that's missing was dinner for a bunch of angry vampires. Here's a news flash for you—you're not that important."

"Krysztof mentioned he didn't have a philosopher—"

"Like anyone needs a philosopher."

"—and here I am not being able to graduate—"

"So, you are blaming me?"

"I don't know who else to blame. I'm being set up, and it is my belief that you never wanted me to become human again. You always wanted me to be a vampire."

"You selfish jerk! I have been working my ass off for you. I've been trying to help you with whatever you decided. This isn't about me. This has always been about you. How dare you accuse me of not being sincere?"

She was only inches away from me. I could see the full extent of this anger. It had stung, the things I said, that I would accuse her of such things. But I had to be right. I had to be.

I looked at her directly in the eyes, feeling dead inside for the trick being played. "I feel so stupid for caring about you."

Without a blink I swear her eyes turned to fire and I felt a hot slap on my face, so hard my glasses flew off and hit the table. Even with my new skin I could feel the sting.

"You should feel stupid." I thought she would rip me to shreds. Instead, Nadia turned, grabbed her things, and left.

As she moved through the door, I saw Beth sitting not a far distance away. She had been listening the whole time.

"Are you kidding me?" I sank my shoulders in frustration. "Nadia!" I tried to fit my glasses back on my face and ran after her. She was in the elevator before I could get there.

I turned to see the panicked look on Beth's face.

"What did you hear?"

She looked up at me. "Everything," she choked out.

"Do you believe it?"

Her eyes squinted in an unreadable expression. "No."

"Good," I answered quickly. "You'll be fine then. Okay. So, will you give Warren a message from me?" She didn't answer, but I didn't expect her to. "Tell him I quit," I said and then took off down the stairs.

24

NETWORKING

"WHENEVER, THEREFORE, PEOPLE ARE DECEIVED AND FORM OPINIONS WIDE OF THE TRUTH, IT IS CLEAR THAT THE ERROR HAS SLID INTO THEIR MINDS THROUGH THE MEDIUM OF CERTAIN RESEMBLANCES TO THAT TRUTH."

Nadia was nowhere in sight; she had completely vanished. But as I looked around the hallways, the question came to my mind, should I care? What was I going to say to her if I did find her? I needed to work things out. I needed answers. I looked down at the street below me and tried to separate my thoughts.

The police would find me. They will know I know something about this. I don't have an alibi; I was in my apartment sulking for the last few days. My secret will be out, and then the world will find out about vampires. How could Nadia do this to me?

When I saw all the yellow taxis piled on the street, I hatched a plan. I needed to find out the truth for myself, and to do that

I needed to talk to Krysztof. Without a phone it was even harder, but I didn't care. I felt that he had the answers I was looking for. I needed to call. The closest phone to me… was Sunnie's. She would help me. I felt it might be a good opportunity anyway to talk with her, even if I hadn't formed the words of what I was going to say.

I took off toward her apartment building. The sun still sat high in the sky, and my skin grazed its rays a bunch of times. I felt right about the sun block, but I tried to sink back in the hood of my jacket and threw my hands deep in my pockets as I ran. People stared at my quick pace, but that was one thing I liked about Manhattan, no one really cared who I was or where I ran to, as long as I didn't steal their taxi.

I wound up at her gate and rang the buzzer.

"Hello?" a familiar voice answered, but it wasn't Sunnie's optimistic cheer.

"Mitch?"

"Ollie?"

"What the hell?" slipped out. "What are you doing here?"

"Oliver?" There was Sunnie's voice.

"Let me up. I need to talk to you," I demanded.

"Not if you're—" Mitch started but was cut off by the sound of the buzzer opening the door.

I took the stairs two at a time and was at her door in a matter of seconds.

Mitch stood there in the open door. I didn't say anything, just walked right in.

"Oliver," Sunnie came up to me and tried to give me a hug, but I brushed it away.

"Kay. Explain. What's going on?" I said. I was very calm, but still upset.

Sunnie went back to her couch and sat. "I'm so sorry, Oliver," she started.

"Are you kidding me?" I gestured to Mitch who was looking rather smug. "It's like high school. Mitch always took my girlfriends. I think they just used me to get to him." I sank to the couch in a heap of realization. "I should have figured."

"It really is my fault," Sunnie started. "Can I explain? I couldn't get hold of you, so I called Mitch. I was troubled about everything. But, come on, you know I was never going to be enough for you, even if you become human again, which, honestly, I have a hard time understanding."

"What do you mean?"

Sunnie smiled in her coy way. "It was enough thinking you are a vampire. I can't imagine you not being one now. That's all. Going back would be such a disappointment." She ruffled some of the fringe on her pillow as she talked. "I called Mitch hoping to contact you, but he offered to help. So, he came over and we talked out some things and it turns out we really have a lot in common."

Mitch smirked and sauntered away in the kitchen.

"You are a cool guy and all, really. The idea of a vampire boyfriend is very romantic in novels, but rather hard to deal with in reality. And you're not a very good vampire, no offense."

"Understand," I agreed.

"It is a little too much for me. Mitch helped me feel better by expressing how he feels about it."

"Really?" I forgot that Mitch had feelings. "He expressed stuff?"

"Girls can get you to do weird things," I heard Mitch yell from the kitchen.

Sunnie grinned. "He did. Don't you get it? He lost his best friend to an undead monster. How would you feel?"

That was an interesting question that would take more consideration if she hadn't alluded to me as the undead monster.

"I don't think the reality of it hit for a while, but he's just fine. We can both deal with it separately and together."

I didn't know how it happened, but a wave of relief came through me. My problem had solved itself. All the work up was for nothing. It was amazing.

Sunnie smiled with her eyes, leaned in and whispered. "Nadia is good for you. You need her."

Ah, Nadia… I just crushed that dream, snapped back to reality by the mere utterance of her name. "No. Nadia hates me."

"Man. What did you do this time?" came from the kitchen. Mitch's head popped around the corner.

"Is my face still red from the slap?" I signaled to my cheek.

"That bad, huh?" he returned.

"I'll help you," Sunnie returned. "She's mad, mostly at me anyway, but if she knows that I don't care for you like that, I think we could be friends."

"Not such a good idea at the moment," I returned. "Let's not play matchmaker so soon after you broke my heart. I need your help with something else first."

My mind had returned to what brought me here in the first place. I quickly explained what had just happened and how that might help.

"Do you still have Brandon's car?" Sunnie yelled to Mitch.

Mitch came out of the kitchen with a hand full of chips. He had ditched my Dorito-less apartment to mooch here, which suited him better anyway. "Oh yeah. He doesn't know I'm back in town yet."

Sunnie grabbed my arm. "Well, let's go then."

"I think it would be faster to hop on the train," I mentioned. Traffic was always difficult, and parking was expensive.

"Let him drive." Sunnie slipped on her shoes and grabbed sunglasses. "I want to ride in it like a movie star."

We were out the door in five minutes.

Sunnie and Mitch filled me in on how everything unfolded the past few days while I sat in my cocoon of an apartment. Mitch said he even felt bad how things had happened.

"I know I've stolen girls from you before, but that was all about sport and competition," he stated. "This one's different. I really didn't expect this one."

I could see the surprise still on his face. If that was Mitch apologizing sincerely, I would accept it. Anything was better than nothing.

"Did you know she figured out the secret code to Code of Honor 4 on the fourth level? I was so impressed."

And there was my selfish best friend back. "You've been playing video games the whole time?"

"Well, not the whole time," he mentioned. "We did need to eat here and there." I laughed at his attempt at humor in a not so humorous environment.

I couldn't help but be impressed by how much Mitch had changed. I can't say changed was the right word for it, he still had his jerky qualities, still self-centered, but possible, instead of living through life, he had found a reason to get up and make something out of his day. Probably not. It had only been a few days.

The Cell in the daylight was nothing more than an abandoned storehouse overlooking the Hudson River, where in Hollywood anything illegal could conspire. I ran around the building trying to find an entrance. Mitch and Sunnie looked near the front of the building. The steel doors were shut tight.

"What do I do?" I talked to myself. I resulted to banging.

"Krysztof!" I shouted. "Krysztof! I know you're in there!" I waved at a few security cameras. "I need your help! Oliver Brixby!"

A side door opened into black. There was no one there.

"Should we go in?" Sunnie hesitated.

"You guys don't have to," I answered.

"Yes, we do," Mitch said, and he took Sunnie's shoulder and pushed her forward. "I can't miss this. This is going to be fun to watch." His smile and anticipation made me uneasy.

I walked into the dark with Mitch and Sunnie behind me. It was completely dark except for the light outside filtering through the door. It slammed shut without warning. The sound echoed loud through the large emptiness.

"Mister Brixby." The voice echoed around the vast, empty room, the same low German accent I remembered.

"Krysztof?"

"You'll have to excuse me. It's very early," a small light lit up at the end on the room, like a cigarette. "Your friends shouldn't be here."

I suddenly felt fear. I forgot about how other vampires were not like me—the passive anti-vampire. "Sorry, sir, they provided me a ride."

"Take them," he said to no one. A big bang thundered near me accompanied by shuffling feet.

"Hey! What the—" Mitch said from behind. There as a scuffle and a yell. I reached around, but they were gone.

"What are you doing?"

"Follow me, Mr. Brixby," and the footsteps led out of the room.

I wasn't sure what to think. I didn't expect there to be any aggressive actions. It took my brain a minute to process everything. I was all alone in this dark room. I fumbled forward. The silhouettes of objects began to stand out along with an outline of a door in front of me.

A large room lay beyond the door, lit with eerie candlelight. Long purple silk lined the walls and lush furniture filled the room. It was much like the room I had first been in when I passed out. Krysztof sat in a large wingback chair looking at me.

"Do you have something to talk to me about?"

"What did you do with my friends?" I asked before anything else.

"I didn't want them hurt," he returned. "I had security lead them to a safe room."

"Seems that you forced them."

"True, it may seem that way," he said as he sipped a wine glass of dark blood. "Your friend Mitchell is very loyal to you. He was most determined to be with you, but I couldn't let him."

"So, they are okay?"

"We shall see," he mused. "Now, you have awoken me at a very early hour. This must be important. How can I be of service?"

I wasn't sure where to start, so I started from the beginning. "Sir, my professor is missing—"

"I think the word you need is dead."

"What?"

"You mean dead, don't you?"

"Well, I just thought he was missing."

Krysztof chuckled a little. "No, my boy, he is dead. I took care of that one personally." He tinged the wine glass with his finger.

"You killed him?"

"Well, of course," Krysztof returned in a lazy manner. "If we don't kill them, we create more of us, and I wouldn't want this man coming back." He leaned forward. "Sorry, but he had a rather bad character. I really didn't think it would turn this way. I thought I was being very reasonable."

"What did you do to him?"

"I don't know if it's polite to ask."

My mind began to spin. "Sorry, could you back up a little? How did you know about all this?"

Krysztof took another sip and then flexed his boney fingers as he sat. "You are assuming that I tampered with your schooling, which I hardly touched. You are a very good student. I just looked into things at the school. The Network is very efficient. We all took an instant like to you. Your story is tremendously entertaining to our dull society."

"The Network?"

"Yes, full of close, personal friends, in various, strategic places. I presumed Nadia would have told you this."

The mention of Nadia made my stomach tighten. "So, you have been spying on me."

"Zu erkunden mit liebe," he muttered. "Spy is a terrible word. Checking up on you is much more appropriate. It was not with intent to hurt, but to improve your life. This is what I do. I am the director. My, you are very entertaining." He broke into a chuckle.

"I'm glad you find me amusing," I remarked. "Explain to me this network."

"Oh, tish. I can't do that." He began swirling his drink again.

I tried to think of what vampires I knew so far. "Was Jovanny in on this?"

"Jovanny is an excellent hacker. I've had access to various things. But only on a need-to-know basis. I only wanted to meet and talk with your professor. It was unfortunate he didn't want to cooperate. I was being very reasonable."

"Reasonable? I really have no idea what that means."

Krysztof half-smiled. "Well, when people hear of our network, there are only two ways to react. His isn't the kind you want. I approached him about placing you in a networking position. Having a connection at a college in the center of Manhattan is an intriguing idea. We gave him many options, all of which he would not participate with."

My face was all sorts of confused. "I wish I had been in on that decision."

"I'm sorry I cannot offer you a place in our network yet." He gulped a big swallow. "Maybe next time."

My mind wrapped around everything Krysztof had said. I sank down on the couch nearest him. "Help me figure out what I need to tell the police?"

"Why?"

"Well, the police will be called."

"Why?" he grinned at me again. "Oh, your naïve, simple ideas of the world."

"People will wonder."

"Why would they?" he probed. "I think you are forgetting what you are. The world no longer runs on the rules that govern the regular population. You need to step in your new world and look at it from the inside out. You will see colors you never knew existed."

A lot of the words he spoke I didn't follow, but I considered something else. I was treating my vampirism like a disease I could overcome, but the reality of it, "Oliver Brixby, deal with it, you're a vampire," regardless of my taste. I couldn't live like a small-town New Jersey College Student anymore. I needed to grow up into my new place in the night as a networking, everyday vampire in New York.

The words in my head didn't match my heart. What if I didn't want to be one of Krysztof's spies? What was I going to do?

"What about my treatment tonight?" I said, thinking about the risky alternative to vampirism.

Krysztof laughed harder than before. "Oh, this is my favorite part. Andrus told me all about it. I think it is a brilliant idea. I doubt it will work, but I'm intrigued by the failure of it. Nadia's foolhardy attempt at bringing you back to LIFE is full of entertainment."

"You like misery, don't you?"

Krysztof straightened up. "I am a vampire. I enjoy many things; human suffering happens to be one of them."

Point taken.

He stood up. It was a hint that my time with him was up. "Are there any more questions?"

I just sat in a stupor. "I guess not."

"And if you are curious, your boss was not very co-operative either."

"Warren?"

"Yes, he was so unreasonable when I talked to him about changing your hours for medical reasons. Medical reasons should justify any condition. It put me in a sour mood, and I happened to see him coming out of a café the other night. I admit that one was a little fun." The weird gleam in his eye made me shiver.

"I guess I should thank you."

"No thanks needed. I didn't do it for you. Now, let us go find your friends."

I stood and followed him back through a few hallways to a room separated by curtains. Mitch was lying down on a bed with a needle in his arm.

"Hey there," he hailed to me. I waved back, relieved they hadn't killed him too. "Thought I might help your cause," he said while pumping a ball in his fist.

"You're donating blood?"

"Red Cross won't take mine because of my time in Europe, but these people won't care."

"Wow," I slipped. "Thank you. You're a changed man. Where's Sunnie?"

"She couldn't donate, so I think she is back talking to Strawberri."

"Strawberri?" I said and then it dawned on me. Ah, right! Strawberri!

A nice-looking woman came and checked Mitch's progress. "Wow, six-minute draw time. Good job."

"Thanks," Mitch uttered as she slipped out the needle and wrapped a bandage around his arm for pressure.

"Here. Eat a banana," she offered him.

"Sure thing," Mitch returned, splitting the banana with his teeth as he stood up. He sat up regaining himself before he led me out to another room just adjacent to the other.

"Oh, I loved it," I overheard. "There are elements to her writing style that is so easy to understand, and the romantic expressions are so real and familiar."

"Thank you," came another sweet little voice say. It was Strawberri Jones, still looking sickly and malnourished, but better than crazed and angry. She saw me and froze.

"How is Krysztof treating you?" I asked as nicely as possible.

She nodded as an okay.

"Don't worry about him," Sunnie said, smiling like the first day I met her. "I was telling her about some books I had just read about a girl that didn't know she was a vampire, and I thought she might like them or relate to them."

"Well," I replied. "I met Sunnie in a paranormal part of the library, so I would take her word for it." I didn't know what else to say. "I hope that we can at least be friends."

"You want to be my friend?" she muttered.

I know it felt strange to say to the girl that ruined my life, but it wasn't me if I didn't get over that part. "Yes, I do."

"Why?"

Her question was honest. "Because I understand your pain and…" I stumbled at what I really wanted to say. "I don't like being angry. I've been angry far too much lately. It's not like me to be angry. I want to help people. That's what I have always wanted to do."

She looked rather bewildered at my response, but there may have been a smile there somewhere.

"Well, it looks like a happy reunion," Krysztof remarked when he found us in the waiting area. "Now, if you would please excuse me, I'm returning to bed. Ty will escort you out." He motioned to the tall man standing behind him. I recognized him as the bouncer at the door of the club.

"Wait," I stopped him before he left. "I need to get in contact with Andrus."

"Hmmm… Ty give him your phone."

Without a second thought, Ty reached into his suit jacket and handed me his sleek touch screen. "You break it, I break you."

It was the first time he had spoken to me. His voice was deep, full, and frightening. I wasn't going to mess with this guy and I slipped the phone gently in my pocket.

"Ty has all the network contacts," Krysztof added. "But dealing with him is like taking on a full-grown gorilla. Just a warning."

I understood his message loud and clear.

25

A CONNECTION TO DARWIN

"THE NEAREST WAY TO GLORY IS TO STRIVE
TO BE WHAT YOU WISH TO BE THOUGHT
TO BE."

I decided to take the subway back home. Mitch and Sunnie offered to give me a ride, but I wasn't ready to spend any more time with them than I had to.

The walk would do me good. I found my way to Greenwich Avenue and sauntered through the street looking in the windows of all the shops. The sun had moved, and most of the shapes gathered on the left side, and if I stayed in the shade of the shop umbrellas, I felt pretty good. The walk felt perfect, and it gave me time to reflect on things.

First, I was living in two worlds: human and non-human, real and unbelievable, and because of it I felt schizophrenic. I kept my hope on becoming human again, but come on, what was the likelihood of that? My body was different than it had been, and Nadia had made some very good points that I kept at the back of my mind: even if I did become a human again, would I want that old life back? Was the life I lived worth saving?

Obviously, I liked myself better as a vampire—my confidence and correspondence had increased tenfold. But I still wasn't a normal vampire either. The reality of it still gave me a pit in my stomach. Could I kill someone? Could I make someone *breakfast*? The thought of Krysztof with the bloody martini of my old professor made my insides turn. Not something I'd soon forget. This lifestyle was different, an adjustment. It had changed me, and my mixing the two worlds so far had not been successful.

With school over, the human side could disappear, and I could go off and live in a castle in Germany, killing only fresh virgins that I seduce and filling the villagers with dread. That image, honestly, was the only image I could conjure of the vampire lifestyle. It was either that or return to the human side and live out my sad life in my parent's basement.

My whole life I had lived with the threat of something happening to me. I preserved myself in a bubble thinking of possibilities that may or may not happen. My preventative nature helped me cope with aspects I never wanted to deal with; this problem couldn't be solved with drugs. There was nothing I could take to help this. I had to completely get out of the routine of taking the morning pills. I depended on them fixing my problems and then I wouldn't need to fix them myself. Here, I was completely dry of pills in my system and had to solve all my problems without stimulants helping me forget how broken I was.

And that was a frightening future.

A dress shop sat on the corner before I crossed, and out of the corner of my eye I saw a long black dress. I stopped and stared. The sight of it hit my memory. It wasn't exactly like

Nadia's dress, nothing compared to that creation she would wear to Vaughn's event. The memory, both sweet and piercing, of Nadia's bare back in that gown opened the flood of everything I had tried so hard not to think about. I didn't want to think about her and feel the pitiful shame and humiliation I felt. I didn't, however, have proof that she was involved. It was the best conclusion at the time. Nadia had to be involved with the network and getting Fessinger killed. Krysztof more or less said it. Right?

But what about thinking like a vampire. I haven't yet. I didn't think I could. If Nadia thought like a vampire, I couldn't fault her. She was too smart to do something without willingly rationalizing the benefits. Maybe it all stemmed from jealousy. Maybe the possibility of me changing back to a human was too amazing and she had to make sure that didn't happen. Or maybe she wanted the glory of it.

I stopped mid-thought at the bottom of Penn Station. "What am I thinking?" I said out loud to no one. An older couple nearly ran into me because I stopped walking. You don't stop in New York, that was the first lesson I learned. "So, sorry." I apologized but grabbed the beautiful gray-haired lady by the shoulders. "She would never do something like that to me. I know it."

The gentleman with her, in his ancient bowler hat huffed at me. "I hope not." He scurried his sweet wife away from me as fast as possible.

How did I let my rambling thoughts rule my logic?

"Maybe it wasn't her." Again, talking to no one.

Nadia had connections throughout the vampire population I couldn't imagine, people I have never met. Then I flashed to our conversation last night. If she wasn't involved, I could

only think of one other who might play a role in this . . .
Jovanny.

And that's when the lightning struck down on me. How
had I missed this? It was obvious. Guilt could be an excellent
maneuvering point. Nadia said making him a vampire was the
worst thing she had done. Jovanny knew she cared for me.

"Do you really think I could be a threat?" The man playing
the guitar at the station nodded to me like he agreed. I reached
into my pocket to find him any spare dollars and rubbed
against the borrowed phone. I pulled it out along with two
bucks which I threw in the case.

I slid open the screen and thought I would do some
investigating. I had never invaded another person's phone
before. Phones are such private things. Unlocking someone's
phone was opening their diary. It felt really wrong to do. I
fumbled around the navigation. Ty's phone was much more
sophisticated than my outdated piece of technology. I looked
through his contact list. It was incredible how long it was. I
finally found Jovanny Moretti along with Nadia.

My stomach flipped with all sorts of nerves as I opened the
last messages sent, all of which were very short and
nondescript, and truly not very helpful. There were a few from
Jovanny from the past weekend, but they didn't mean
anything to me:

> *— Frederick Phineas was a lucky man. —*

> *— I need to find a blood walnut. —*

> *— Pot stickers sound delicious tonight. —*

> *— All daring and courage all iron endurance of
> misfortune make for a finer nobler type of manhood.
> —*

I had no idea what these meant, so I checked out on his Google app and typed in Blood Walnut. It popped open a tree image and a ton of news stories. I scrolled down on the page and saw a picture with a map of Central Park. I clicked on it, and it led me to a news story about 100 new trees planted in Central Park, including the Blood and Black Walnut tree. I didn't think I was going in the right direction and scrolled back up to search for something else.

The pot sticker text was too vague to search, but I had no idea who Frederick Phineas was, so I searched for him. The search engine brought up a few obituaries, I skimmed the headlines until I read something very interesting. This couldn't be a coincidence. I read on…

"…will be held in the Frederick Phineas and Sandra Priest Rose Earth and Science Center located at the Museum of Natural History in New York…"

I took better notice at the data from the algorithm. Many of the articles talked about the famed building of this Philanthropist benefactor. I got chills and I wasn't sure why.

I went back to the search bar and typed in the first lines, "All daring and courage all iron endurance…"

The first thing that popped up was a quote from Theodore Roosevelt. I hit images and scrolled down. There it was—a large plaque with these words among others inscribed at the American Museum of Natural History here in New York.

Umm… I just stumbled on a code, a very dangerous one. There would be no other reason for speaking in such code unless it was dangerous. People might find out. I stopped in a brief moment of clarity—like me. And things were kept from me. Why? And now nothing added up.

I had hit a moment of bravery. Before I knew it, I stepped on the subway heading toward the Museum of Natural History.

I took out Ty's phone again as I rumbled along and looked over the texts again.

I hit reply.

– Darwin was right –

Was all I wrote and hit send.

I got a response almost instantly…

– Be there in 10 –

I had no idea what I started. Be where in ten? What was I meaning to do? I began to panic. I found Nadia's contact and began a new message.

- What does Jovanny want with you –

I thought I was being smart since she couldn't track the phone, thinking it was Ty sending it to her and not me. How courage can make us fools. It took a minute before I got the response.

– He's trying to mess with Oliver –

– Explain this to me – I wrote. I tried to be in Ty's mind and channel his voice in my head, but I had only heard him speak once.

Beep! *– It's just part of his games. Jovanny is a bully and found a target –*

– What are you going to do? –

Beep! – *Pray Jovanny gives up. He's afraid I'm falling for Oliver and not him. –*

What? I thought in my head. I felt guilt, yet it was sweet guilt. I was getting out secrets, but she would kill me if I knew.

Beep! – *I thought Krysztof knew. Shouldn't you be protecting Mitch? –*

What was she talking about Mitch for?

– *He and the girl are fine* – I texted back.

I waited for a text, but it didn't come. Instead, the phone rang. "Sh—!" I fumbled to push silent, then stuffed the phone back into my pocket and continued holding on to the rail.

Several minutes later I arrived at 81st street and stepped out to a large, tiled dinosaur on the wall. I had always meant to come to the Museum. It was almost mandatory for an anthropology minor to come here; I guess I failed there too. Manhattan seemed so big, until I came here and discovered it's just a place.

The platform looked very bare. The entrance to the museum from the tunnel had closed, so I followed the stream of bodies exiting up the stairs. When I arrived at the top, the sun was on the other side of the buildings.

I looked at the building; big banners with large frogs, and what I thought was a Gila monster, billowed down the ancient front of the museum. The archway was enormous like a large cathedral. I looked at my watch. It was about 5:30. The museum closed to the public at 5:45, but I went to buy a ticket anyway.

"But we are about to close," the girl at the desk said.

"Yes, I know, but I think I left my jacket in there," I lied. "Can I just run in and check."

"Where do you think you left it?"

"By the apes," I returned.

"By the primates or by the Origins of Man," she asked inquisitively.

"Origins, definitely," I stated. I must have looked charming as I added a tiny flip to my eyebrow, because she smiled and winked me past. What a strange and unusual power lying is as a vampire.

I looked at a map and headed in what I thought was the direction to the Origins exhibit. I did get a little distracted at the enormity of the museum. I really needed to come back here one day, when I had more time, and the possibility of my friends' lives weren't in danger.

Then without a mistake I found the Hall of Origins. It was an enormous display of skeletons, fossils, Neanderthals, and a huge DNA strand. The amount of information was astounding. I found myself transfixed reading some of the information displayed on a plaque when a voice behind me grabbed my attention.

"Don't you know the museum is about to close?"

I turned and who did I expect but Jovanny. And not only him, but a large man in a gray suit, and behind him was Ty accompanied by Mitch and Sunnie. This was a strange reunion.

"What are you doing here?" I asked. My question was directed mostly to Mitch.

"A test," Jovanny said with a big grin on his face. "I think you're doing well."

I didn't understand but went with it. "Because I figured out your clues?" I said as I held up the phone.

"Yep," Jovanny returned, like he didn't care.

"Am I being graded?"

Jovanny looked. "Not really. It's more of a pass/fail kind of thing," he smoothed out. "And I kinda cheated. Ty told me you had his phone. And this is really tough for me, because I really want to like you. I have to give you some kind of credit for surviving this long as, whatever it is that you are."

"Thanks?" I questioned. "Friends of yours?" I meant vampires.

"I do have a lot of friends," Jovanny stated. "I'm a very likable guy, you know."

"I'm sure you are, so you don't need to worry about me then. I'll just ask that you let my friends go, and we'll all be fine."

Jovanny wasn't letting up. I kept rambling. "I liked you when we first met, actually—even the second time. I play a good rogue if ever you want to play D&D, but yeah, I'm not sure if I should like you now."

Jovanny smiled. "Yeah, I don't know how I can change that. Sorry."

"I meant to thank you for finding the girl," I commented, hoping to distract him.

"Thrill of the hunt, and I didn't really do it for you. It was just part of my plan."

"Don't they have cameras here?" I asked.

"Nope, not right now at least."

This talk was tedious. "So, are you going to kill me now?"

"No," he smiled. "But I think you should kill these guys." He pointed to Mitch and Sunnie, who I hadn't noticed were tied and gagged.

"What? Why?" I started in utter confusion. "There is nothing to prove."

"It proves to me that you are an equal and viable advisory."

"Yeah, but can't we just spar on the green like you do with all the rest of your role playing? That is what you're doing, isn't it?"

"That's not as fun," he snorted. "I'm testing your willingness to the cause"

I felt my bravery coming, something I never had before, unless you were the waiter that brought me out the Garza salad with the dressing on the top and not on the side. I became very brave that day. "I know this doesn't have to do with them. What do you really want from me?"

"Easy. Stay away from Nadia."

"Done!" I shouted. "By the way, she hates me. Did I mention that?"

"I doubt that," Jovanny stated. "Nadia is not yours. She's mine. That's how this works. Promise me you'll stay away."

A wave of her silky black hair came back into my mind, and I took a deep breath. "I can't do that." And he knew that was the truth. "But let me share something with you. You can't bully people into loving you."

"It's worked pretty well for me so far."

"But it doesn't work with Nadia." I poked a sore spot. Anger raged in his face. I started to regret what I had said. These were real vampires, not like me. Whatever face they wore before was not what they were capable of. He walked up close to me until he stood only a few feet away. I gulped, but the courage came anyway. "I think Nadia has cared for you the best she can. I think she tried, but guilt is not the best way to win her affection."

"She changed me," he said with tension in his voice.

"If it wasn't her, it would have been someone else. Someone else you could make do whatever you want."

I didn't see it coming, but the punch came right at my jaw and knocked me sideways. I'm sure I would have had a bloody nose if I could bleed. This was an interesting moment. Yes, I had been punched, and yes, it still stung even without a pulse. But the action cleared away doubt and fear, and I felt a surge of energy ripple inside my non-human body. I had only really been in one fight in my life and that was with Mitch. He wasn't my best friend at the time, but he was now, and he stood helplessly tied up near the Stages of Life. I learned I didn't like being bullied or that I can turn situations around. No. I learned that as much as I detest fighting, I am not as bad at fighting as most people think.

As the punch sent me sideways, an angry vein flashed somewhere inside, and I thought and acted like a vampire should. And just as I got to my feet, I moved with swiftness and came at him with my head right to his stomach, punching furiously at anything I could hit.

I can't remember much of what happened—a lot of punching, smacking, tumbling into glass filled with naked Neanderthals. I felt every punch, and though my body didn't feel the soreness and ache as I would being human, it was not pleasant, and I knew I wasn't going to spring back from this easily. Finally, as I stumbled in front of a Plexiglas case of someone named Lucy, he hit me in the back with such force that I fell and chipped the side of the display.

I think he felt satisfied.

I grabbed onto a rail and pulled myself up. My head felt weird; a continuous ringing echoed around and around. My body felt stiff and uncomfortable. I looked around and saw no other escape. Mitch struggled; Sunnie was trying to scream. I decided to dig into my education and talk.

I looked at him with a big grin on his face, a near perfect sneer on his lip. "Are you happy?"

"I feel pretty good, yeah," he returned rubbing around his shoulders.

"What great significance does this have on you?"

He looked at me with a dumb expression. "Leveling your ass feels pretty good."

"But it doesn't solve the problem," I returned. I now stood taller with a clear mind. "All you do is pretend. That is all you have done. That is all you know. I lived a full life, and I have family and friends supporting me the entire time. I never imagined it, it was real, and I am grateful for it. I never needed to pretend I was loved. I still am loved and will continue to be."

"Skip the melodrama!" Jovanny yelled at me.

"A vampire doesn't change overnight. It won't make you more liked or more loved. Don't you get that?"

"Shut up, Brixby!"

I knew I was getting to the heart of the problem, and as I spoke it out loud, it made more sense to me. "Being a vampire is just another allergic kid in the back row. You're the kid that can't eat the snickers bar because of the peanuts. But there is a difference—you chose to be allergic to peanuts and I didn't. You wanted a peanut allergy. Who asks for that? This path wasn't what I ever expected, but I know how to deal with it. I know how to curb a craving and avoid the tantalizing. Now you don't know what to do with yourself."

"You are talking nonsense," Jovanny yelled. "I don't need your idiotic, psychotic babble."

"I'm a philosopher—big difference."

"Whatever," he threw out. "It means the same to me."

"Do you know what one of the questions philosophers haven't solved?" I asked. "What's the meaning of life? Well, I think I figured out something today. Life doesn't have to have a pulse. I'm not going to stop living. Don't throw it out thinking you can be something better; don't waste your life pretending to be someone else. Be true to what you are."

It was silent for a moment until an alarm sounded and security rushed in. Quickly everyone was surrounded and began to be escorted out. A man with a tweed jacket and beard came over to me accompanied by a security guard.

"Keep him here," the man instructed. "I'd like to talk to him."

The guards obeyed, and soon the hall was empty, except for me and this man.

"I'm Bill Blood," he introduced himself. "I am the curator here at the museum."

I remained silent. I didn't know how much trouble I was in.

"Krysztof tells me you are about to graduate."

"How do you know Krysztof?" I asked, but then thought it was a stupid question—Krysztof knew everyone.

Bill grinned slightly. "Krysztof has helped me out of a jam," he stated, but our eyes connected, and I understood more than I thought. "Let me explain something to you." He motioned to walk with him. "Loyalty has always been more important than secrecy, you understand?"

"I guess."

"Mr. Ty was the plant, and Mr. Moretti was the bait," he sighed. "But our dear mutual friend asked me to watch you in this particular confrontation."

"How did he know what I would do?"

The man laughed in his throat—not a joyful sound, but a cynical laugh that was not at all friendly. He didn't answer my question. "But back to my question, you are graduating from Hunter."

I nodded.

"Can I suggest something to you?" he said. I wasn't going to say no. "Stick with what you love."

I stopped walking and looked at him.

"Do you see what I do?" he asked, but I wasn't following his question. He gestured to the large room we were now in. An enormous blue whale hung from the ceiling. "I could have done something else you know. Something more glamorous, but I *choose* to stay here." He continued walking without saying another word.

Choosing. A choice.

When we reached his office, only Mitch and Sunnie were there. "Are you all okay?" I asked.

"Of course," Mitch returned. "But when Ty asked us for our help, I didn't think it would hurt so much." He was rubbing his wrist.

"It was all an act?"

"It depends," Sunnie entered the conversation. "Are you still planning on killing us?"

"Not yet," I mentioned. "Where's Jovanny?"

"I had police take him for a few days," Bill mentioned as he grabbed his jacket. "Destruction of property. Lucy is one of our most valued treasures." He added a wink. "If you don't mind, the museum is now closed. Time for you all to leave."

26

THE BOATHOUSE GALA

"LIFE CONTAINS BUT TWO TRAGEDIES. ONE IS NOT TO GET YOUR HEART'S DESIRE; THE OTHER IS TO GET IT."

I returned home and checked my body. How could I get such deep bruises when I didn't have any blood? But then I remembered my procedure with Elle and I panicked.

Did I mean what I said today to Jovanny? If I did, then what? Should I try the experiment, or should I deal with my life as it is? I tried to think about who I was before I was bit. I thought of sushi, but it really wasn't any different than some of the items I had in my fridge now.

I looked through what I had bought earlier and decided to try and make something to eat. I remember willingly making the choice to be a vegetarian. This wasn't much different. But I was getting sick of smoothies, so I tried a recipe Nadia gave me for something called Czernina: a soup made with duck blood and Nadia modifications. It was delicious and just what my body needed.

The procedure with Elle kept haunting me. I needed to leave and get this done. Why was I still sitting on the couch?

What did I really want? Would I regret it if I didn't go? Yes. But all that I said to Jovanny about accepting yourself, and there I would go and try to change it. But I'm only trying to return what was stolen.

Choosing. A choice.

Then I thought about all the friends I had made. What about them? What about little Strawberri and her new idea of life as a vampire? Who was going to watch out for her?

Unintentionally, I made my decision and rolled over and went to sleep.

I woke to a noisy horn down on the street. I looked out and it was midday and overcast. I felt refreshed and happy. Happy. When was the last time I had been happy? My cynical side wasn't here this morning. I didn't feel my burdens so heavy today.

I finished off the rest of the soup and took a long-needed shower. The water was cold and stung a little. I liked it. When I stepped out, I checked out the damage to my body. I looked polka dotted. The punches were black. I wondered why that happened. They didn't hurt, but I felt stiffer than usual. Even on my face, the jawline punch left a black mark like a tire track skid mark. I guess that would be what I would tell people if anyone asked. I just got my face run over.

Afterward, I brought out my computer and found a message from the office of the Administrator of Affairs at Hunter College stating all matters have been resolved with my impending graduation.

Well, okay then. This is it. My new life was beginning. Refreshed as I had never been before, I set out with a new outlook and prepared myself for what I might do with my new decision.

I headed into the city. I thought I would stop by the Apple store and buy a new phone, and it happened to be in the same direction as somewhere else, a place that had been on my mind. Before I knew where I was, I walked in the Wexler Library. I greeted a few people as I headed up to the second floor where I saw Beth typing away. She glanced up and then went back to her typing, though her keystrokes were not as precise as before.

"Can we talk?" I asked. Though, as I thought about it, I didn't know what I was going to say.

"Umm, sure," she returned, but it sounded like a question.

I moved around the desk and sat next to her. She was still busy, but I saw her tremble. I moved my hand out and stopped her typing. She sat there still for a moment before she looked up at me. In her eyes I saw the terror.

"I quit, you know that," I stated.

"Yes, I am aware."

I smiled and tried to lighten up the mood. "I really want to be your friend."

She nodded, but her look softened.

"You'll still be my friend? Promise?" I questioned her expression.

"Sure, if that is what you want."

"I'm trying to still figure out everything," I stated without really thinking about anything. "This is all new to me, and I tried to continue being who I was before, and I can't. It's not possible. But I wanted you to know, you are not in any danger."

Beth's face turned curiously toward me. "Really? But I know what you are. I know you might have." She gulped and I patted her hand.

"Hazards of the food chain," I said, lighthearted. "But I am not like that, and I promise you are not in any danger as long as I am your friend. Understand?"

She looked me over and returned a nod.

"Would you be willing to help me if I asked for it?"

"Certainly," she returned. "Do you need anything?"

"Not now, but it might be good to have a smart girl like you on my side. And I miss coffee. Find out if there is anything from Starbucks that I might be able to drink. There has to be some kind of blend."

She squinted in a quirky manner trying to figure out my meaning but couldn't. She gave a shoulder shrug. "I'm your girl for that. Anything you need, Ollie, just let me know."

Deborah, the cat lady, moved across the floor and saw me. "Well, my stars in heaven," she stated and moved over to greet me. "Good to see you. Oliver, you need to come meet Lemon Peel. She is a sweetheart and loves to be cuddled."

"I'll try," I said as I moved up out of her seat and headed downstairs again. "Take care," I turned with a wave.

I caught Beth's smile. It wasn't a real smile, but a sympathetic smile, but it was a smile still.

I got my new phone, and the nice people transferred my number and charged it for me. When I got to my messages I had so many and started scrolling through as I walked. It had been a crazy few days and a lot of the messages had been resolved. The newest ones were from Elle Vann wondering where I was and if I was okay.

I texted her back.

> *— Sorry I didn't come last night. Complications*
> *came up. Don't reschedule. Talk about it later. —*

I didn't receive a reply for a while, but it was a quick…

> *— K —*

I figured she wasn't very happy, but it would work out.

I looked through more texts and missed called messages from my mother and on and on.

But there was no message from Nadia.

I had completely lost track where I was walking, and I looked up and saw I was across the street from Vaughn Ohlstrom's shop. I ran over and went in.

The shop during the day was a bustling boutique. I went to the counter and asked for Vaughn.

"I'm sorry. He is very busy," she said not caring about my request at all.

"Please, I must see him. He has to be around."

"Sorry. He is preparing for the VO Gala and is not available."

The Gala. That was it. That was my answer.

"Can you at least direct me to his special section?" I asked.

The girl eyed me very carefully and then took me over to a corner of the store that had very fine suits and shirts. They looked like everything else I had seen at Macy's but a lot more expensive.

The next week went by without any problems. I contacted my parents who were excited about coming to my graduation. It was good to hear from them and have their support, whether they believed me or not.

I also hung out with Mitch and Sunnie, and it was a good thing. I could see the good that was happening to Mitch. Sunnie was a very cool person to have around. She got Mitch's jokes, and they could talk the same gaming code that I never really understood. As a human, Sunnie was ideal, but as a non-human, it would never work. I was okay with that.

I tried to get a hold of Nadia, but she would never return my calls. I figured that she hated me anyway, but at the moment it didn't matter.

My graduation went fantastic, if I can call it that. Commencement was held in the Javits North Building at 1:00

p.m., but it was inside, and everything went well. I even smiled a few times. I sat next to David Littlelight and a few other philosophy majors. He never looked at me or talked to me about anything that happened on the day Dean Fessinger disappeared.

They talked very briefly about that too. A letter was read that he had resigned for health issues and didn't want to discuss it further. I felt fine with that explanation.

After Commencement, I met my family, a few of my distant relatives, my Nana, and Mitch who came with Sunnie. We went to dinner afterward, which I found ahead of time called Valencia's Family Italian. Krysztof mentioned it to me when I talked to him about my family coming for graduation. There was a cook that was on his side of things and prepared something he hoped I could tolerate. And though I was still sensitive to certain components in a vampire diet, I tolerated more than I expected. The food prepared for me I only messed around with, but the drink was fabulous. It's funny how easily blood can look like Clamato.

It was Friday night, and my family had left. I changed into my suit I purchased from VO and dressed ready to kill, figuratively.

The VO Gala was held at the Boathouse in Central Park. I couldn't believe it when I saw just how magnificent everything looked for the event. I headed toward the security check and hadn't considered they may not let me in. Then I heard my name.

"Oleever!" It was Ludja, the long-legged supermodel I met at the Cell my first week being a vampire. I only met her once. She made a strong impression on me, but I figured she would never remember my name. She came over to me, kissed me on each cheek, and security let me enter.

"Hello," I replied to the gracious greeting.

"But where is Meech?" she asked.

"He couldn't make it tonight."

"Vhat a shame," she returned. "Come over by me."

We traveled to a corner filled with people. I couldn't help but watch the others around me. Were they all vampires? I slid in my pocket and pulled out my sunglasses Vaughn gave me. The majority of the people around me had very little or no Ultraviolet light emanating from their bodies. Nearly all of the serving staff was glowing orange red, and I spotted a few here and there in the company of vampires. I removed them again to see their faces. It was amazing, such a large number of vampires here, and I felt almost nearly like one of them, or imagined I did.

In the corner I met some of Ludja's supermodel friends. Some could easily be vampires, but others I think just liked a good party. After a moment, I excused myself to explore. I passed the refreshment table and grabbed a dessert that looked like a red velvet cupcake. After biting it though, I could feel the wonderful flavor enter my body as I slowly sucked on the moist cake. I couldn't think of anything better...

Until I spotted her—my entire reason for coming.

She stood talking to someone in that same stunning black dress that was such an illusion to me. Fear swept over my body, and I froze. If she saw me staring, what would I do? I felt like a school kid. How long had it been since I had seen her or talked to her? I suddenly felt the hot slap on my face after I had accused her of having my professor over for dinner, in a manner of speaking.

Focus, I said to myself. This is why I came tonight—to talk to her. My feet started moving though my brain hadn't decided what to say. Why was I so nervous? It's only Nadia, in a stunning, backless black dress. Nothing to fear, right? With her hair swept to the side. Was it natural to feel uneasy just thinking her name? *Stay calm, Oliver.*

And then I was right behind her.

The man she was talking to turned to me. "Yes?"

Nadia turned at that same moment and her beautiful face locked eyes with me and turned to utter astonishment. "What are you doing here?"

I didn't know what to say.

"Would you please excuse me, Luis," she said to the man and walked forward across the room. I followed her.

Nadia remained silent. She walked directly outside to a quiet pier overlooking the water and turned around. "What do you want?"

The question was so direct I completely derailed, and all thoughts emptied into a giant puddle in my brain. "I want to apologize. Can I do that?"

She folded her arms and waited.

Ah crap, she wanted an apology. I should have thought about everything first before I spoke, but I couldn't filter out all the different words, it simply started pouring out of me. "I couldn't be sorrier about what happened in the Wexler. I was completely wrong about what I said and did. If I could take back my words, I would. If I had a time machine, I would go back and erase that entire evening and replace it with a candlelight dinner. Please forgive me."

She still waited.

And I waited. What else did she want? I looked deep in her eyes. Such a mistake to do. "I'm struggling processing my thoughts. But I don't know how else to do it. I had no consideration for any different point of view. It was so cowardly for me to turn on you, assuming you had something to do with it. I couldn't rationally think of anywhere else to turn my frustration."

"So, now your human heart wants forgiveness," she spat out. "So, you can live with your decisions."

"I'm not following you," I said, but I shouldn't have said it, because she just rolled her eyes and continued walking around the boathouse and down the path. "No, wait!" I yelled after her.

"It's too late, Parker," she threw her hands in the air. "You had your chance to fix things, and now it doesn't matter anymore."

I caught up to her and grabbed her arm. "Wait a second. Fix what? What doesn't matter?" I could see something in her eyes that I hadn't found before—disappointment.

"Go return to your girlfriend and have a great life," she said without a look at me.

And then it hit me.

"I think I better tell you something." I led her to a bench, and she sat there staring out at the water. "Sunnie and I aren't dating."

Nadia's head lifted to look at anything but me.

"She wasn't really my type," I fidgeted. "She is more Mitch's type."

Nadia understood the meaning and reached out with her hand and touched my knee. "I'm sorry to hear that."

The shock of her playful touch sent sensations everywhere. I reacted as calmly as possible. "And something else, Jovanny punched me in the face."

She turned to me and looked at my face. "Where?"

I pointed out the black mark still on my face.

A tiny smile crept on her face. She moved her hand up to my chin and rubbed the mark gently. "I meant where were you when he punched you?"

"In the Hall of Human Origins," I stated. "About a week ago," I stated. "It's not the only bruise."

"Why would you do that?"

"I wanted him to leave you alone."

"Why?"

"Because you needed to be free."

"But what would possess you to fight him? He could destroy you."

"Believe me, I know," I moved my body in reflex. "A weak moment of bravery. But I realized something during that experience. I needed to make a change in my life, because…" I paused before I continued. "Because, if I wanted you in my life, I needed to make that change."

She shook her head. "Don't go saying that," she muttered. "Our lives are separate. Two different worlds."

"No, they are the same, I promise you."

"Please, Park." Nadia turned away again.

I squared my shoulders and reached deep to find that bravery I talked about. "I didn't go to the procedure. I didn't go."

"What?" Nadia looked back at me. I stared at her eyes again. God, why did she have to be so beautiful? All courage drained again. "Why would you do that?"

"I realized as I fought Jovanny that *you* are worth fighting for." I turned this time. I couldn't watch her anymore. It was too much. "Jovanny was crazy with jealousy. That makes a man feel good. I could win this fight. And I've never won a fight in my life. You liked me just as I am. Not better or bigger. You liked me at the clinic, but I wasn't part of your world. I know you liked it when I entered your world. And you taught me about your life and showed me your world and sincerely tried to help me the entire way. Unselfishly tried to help me. I had to stay in your world. I couldn't not be part of that world. And this undead life is not bad. It's adventurous and interesting and filled with…" My head slighted towards her. "It's filled with you."

Nadia blinked as the impact came to her realization. I waited, studying every reaction.

"Me?"

I nodded. "You saved me. Even in death, you saved me, and I don't want to be in this city without you."

This time I was prepared. She moved quickly toward me and caught her kiss full and hard. I lost all train of rational thought as I investigated how her lips moved. I couldn't think of anything else but her, here with me. I knew I made the right decision.

When she pulled back and looked at me again, I couldn't speak, just stared and lost myself.

Nadia grinned. "Sorry for believing you would leave me."

"What?"

"And to tell you the truth," she wrapped around me tight, "I never liked Sunnie."

I laughed and couldn't help myself and kissed her again with confidence, no longer afraid of what I did with my lips. It felt better than anything in the entire world, anything I could ever imagine. She accepted all my idiosyncrasies and problems. Nadia liked me as I was, and she made me better. I knew living this way would not be easy, but it certainly would be entertaining with someone like Nadia to spend it with.

The bite was worth it.

I'd have to thank Strawberri someday.

ACKNOWLEDGEMENTS

Nothing is more rewarding than hanging around fabulous people saving lives every day. Thank you, my awesome team and BB family, past and present, for all your inspiration, encouragement, guidance, and deep knowledge of laboratory science and love of blood, especially the few I no longer see, but think of always.

Special dedication to Kellie Nelson, Matt Foger, Breyanna Smith, Shirley DeMet, and the fabulous Alisha Viehl, I miss you daily.

Thank you, Cassidy Rapier, for the disgusting experience that sparked the idea. We all know high society vampires would drink platelets.

Big hugs to my very patient husband and family, Momma still loves you; A huge thank you to my team, specifically my editor, Talysa Sainz, for bringing Oliver back to life.

READ MORE FROM
CANDI TEASDALE

Romantic Comedy
TO DREAM IN DAYLIGHT

FANTASY UNDER
CANDACE J. THOMAS

The Vivatera Series
VIVATERA
CONJECTRIX
EVERSTAR

Poetry
WANDERING BEAUTIFUL

CANDI TEASDALE

Find more at: authorcanditeasdale.com

VAMPIRE BY DAY – WRITER BY NIGHT.

Along with authoring, Candi has more than twenty years of laboratory experience working in Transfusion Medicine. This book reflects on how vampire fiction loses its mystique when knowing blood mechanics, which also made it "bloody" good fun to write (pun totally intended).

Candi holds a BA in Creative Writing from SNHU and pens YA Fantasy under Candace J. Thomas. She has won several awards for her fiction, including the Diamond Quill for Novel of the Year. She lives in the Salt Lake Valley with her family, two fluffballs and too many socks.